Duke of Storms

Regency Hearts

Book 4

Jennifer Monroe

Regency Hearts Series

The Duke of Fire

Return of the Duke

The Duke of Ravens

Duke of Storms

Chapter One

At the age of one and twenty, Emma Barrington had learned many lessons in life. One lesson that had caught her attention on more than one occasion was that men had a peculiar habit of scratching their heads. Although, she had not had many encounters with men outside of the bookkeeping services of her father, nor had she paid any particular attention to those she met on the street.

Stephen Foreman, the assistant her father had hired on when Emma was quite young, was at this moment scratching at his head in an absent manner, as if it aided in his thinking. He was not a dirty man, for he did take relatively good care of himself by washing every morning, but his habit of scratching seemed to happen without thought more than to ease an actual itch. She had never seen any crawlers on him, and if she had, she would have sent him off to wash himself from head to toe — twice!

"And what're you finding so funny?" Stephen asked as he stopped scratching his silver-covered head and scrunched his brows in confusion.

"Oh, it is nothing," she said, waving a hand as if to rid herself of her laughter. She doubted he would understand the humor in the situation as she did. Yet, she found she could not stop when he returned his hand to his head.

"You women are a peculiar lot," he replied, stopping his scratching to stare at her once more, which only made her laugh all the harder until tears ran down her cheeks.

She took a deep breath in an attempt to regain her composure. It would not be fitting to be found weeping with laughter if a client happened by, which was what they were wont to do whenever she found herself out of sorts, such as now. Her father was a bookkeeper, a man once highly sought after when times were better. Now, as she sat in her father's chair at his desk, she wondered if times would continue to decline. She certainly hoped not, for if they worsened any further, they would be without any clients within a month's time.

"I can only agree with your observation," she said when she had herself once more under control. "We most certainly are a peculiar lot."

But not as peculiar as you men! she thought as she grasped the ledgers stacked in front of her. "These must be delivered promptly," she said aloud. "No dawdling."

Stephen glanced at the covers. "Ah, these're going to the Duke of Storms, are they?"

Emma narrowed her eyes at him. "It is not proper to speak of him in that manner. The proper name is Lucas Redstone, Duke of Rainierd, and we are to address him as 'His Grace' when we speak of him."

"I'm sorry, Miss Emma," he said, "but he's got a fiery temper; I know firsthand. He's taken it out on me enough times, that's for sure." He rubbed the side of his head — although the duke had never struck him as far as Emma knew — and then sighed. "I didn't mean to disappoint you."

Emma stood and walked around the desk to place a hand on his arm. "You have not disappointed me," she said with a smile. "In fact, you have always done a wonderful job. You are a fine addition to our office, and I am proud to call you my friend."

His cheeks reddened considerably at her words, and he gave her a broad grin. "Thanks, Miss Emma. I appreciate you sayin' so." He picked up the ledgers. "I'll leave now."

He closed the door behind him, and Emma walked over to stare out the window that looked over the slow-moving traffic that ambled through the tiny village of Rumsbury, Wiltshire. Or what was considered a tiny village, for now. Rumors of plans for new buildings were making their rounds, although nothing had been built as of yet.

If every planned building was constructed, the village would become a city as large as Marlborough to the south. Well, perhaps not as large, but the difference would be significant.

Deciding a breath of spring would be a wonderful change from the dusty office, she took a step outside. A light breeze was cool on her arms, brought about by a storm to the west that echoed the tightness in her neck and back. She took a deep breath, enjoying the sweet smells of the nearby woods, and then let it out slowly.

"Ah, Miss Barrington," Mr. Trelling, a tailor by trade who kept his shop three doors down from the Barrington office, called out to her. "How are you this wonderful day?"

"I am very well, thank you," Emma replied. "I believe we are in for some rain." She motioned to the clouds gathering on the horizon.

Mr. Trelling shook his head. "It always rains," he said with a sigh. Then he rubbed his hands together. "Yet, that can also mean a need for more new coats." Then he sighed. "I suppose I should return to my orders." He reached out to open the door and then stopped. "By the way, I'm curious. When's your father returning from his trip?"

Emma gave him a warm smile. "It should be within a week. Would you like that I send him your way when he returns, or do you have a message you would like me to pass along to him?"

"If you'd just let him know that the coat he ordered some time ago is ready, and that I need him to come in for a final fitting when he has a moment, I'd greatly appreciate it." Emma went to speak, but he raised his hand. "No need to hurry; he has already paid."

Emma breathed a sigh of relief. "Thank you," she said, attempting to keep her voice from shaking. "I will inform him as soon as he returns."

Mr. Trelling bid her a farewell once again, entered his shop, and closed the door behind him.

As Emma returned to the office, she thought of her father, and more particularly, his business. He had begun his bookkeeping venture twenty years earlier, just after Emma was born, and his first clients were cobblers, milliners, and other shop owners. Word traveled in short time of his abilities, and soon those of the *ton* were requesting his services.

Although custom had been good enough to place him high in the ranking of bookkeepers in the past, in more recent months the number of clients had been dwindling at a steady pace. Many could no longer afford to pay, and even those of the peerage found their fortunes disappearing, leaving them no choice than to maintain their own books, not to mention those who not only had to sell their homes used only for holidays but their main residences, as well.

As those of title suffered, so did Emma and her father, their earnings so meek, they had been forced to count every farthing.

From a young age, Emma's father had taught her to read and write, and by the age of twelve, she was learning the intricacies of bookkeeping, even remaining awake late in the night with him as he explained every fine detail of the craft. In that training, she learned that her father knew every investment made by every member of the *ton* on his list of clients as well as which investments were lucrative and which were not.

If she were a man, she would have considered taking over for her father one day, invest some of his savings into some of those lucrative ventures, and join the ranks of the wealthy. Women bookkeepers were frowned upon, so, over the past five years, she had aided him with his bookkeeping business in secret. If any of their clients, be he upper or lower class, ever learned how much she had aided in maintaining his books, he would pull his account faster than if he had placed his hand in the fire.

The truth of the matter was she was more than capable in her secret position. She would continue to do what she could in order to keep the business afloat, even if it required her to continue to hide just how much she did contribute.

Sitting at her father's desk, she opened a drawer and removed a small purse. The weight of it excited her. She had saved this money for over a year — going without new slippers and mending every piece of clothing she owned in order to do so — and now it was time to spend it.

***

Emma ignored the sounds of the people passing her in the street as she gazed into the dressmaker's shop. Inside, women of the *ton* milled about, peering into books, touching bolts of a variety of fabrics and ribbons, and walking in and out of doorways draped with curtains.

The dresses these women wore as they made choices for new were far better than anything Emma had ever owned. The fabrics were of the finest quality and the bows were tied to perfection. Even the hats they wore were exquisite, and glancing at her reflection, Emma felt a moment of shame. The dress she wore was well-worn and well out of fashion, if it had been in fashion at any time. The dark blue had long since faded and it lacked any ribbons or bows. Yet it was one of the finest she owned.

Worrying her lip, she felt the weight of the small purse in her hand, which contained all of her savings for a year meant to purchase a new dress. She had dreamed of such a purchase, having little skill with a needle beyond mending and patching. Most of her dresses had been made in exchange for services when finances were low, and even then, never from a shop as important as the one owned by Mrs. Shilvers.

She had also saved enough to buy a pair of gloves and a hat. Not just any hat but one that, when worn with the new dress, would draw the attention of an eligible man.

Of course, it could not be just any man. He would have to be handsome, well-spoken, and enjoy reading poetry as well as show an interest in nature. With this new dress, she would be courted by such a man, and in time fall in love. For the poets spoke of love, something she wished so desperately to experience. To live a life with a man in marriage, a man she could love, to whom she could bear children. Although she had yet to experience love, she was ready for it. When people fell in love, they shared the burdens on their hearts and souls and received comfort and encouragement in return. She would share her dreams — and Emma had many — with the man who won her heart. Once she found love, those dreams would all come true, and nothing would convince her otherwise.

"You have earned this," she whispered in an attempt to stave off the guilt she felt for such frivolity. Money was especially tight as of late, and perhaps it would be better spent in other ways.

Yet, this had been the reason she had saved the money. It had been her dream. Her attention was drawn to a finely dressed couple who wore wide smiles with eyes blazing with the love she knew was in their hearts. Seeing this was confirmation; she was meant to get this new dress.

As she reached out to grasp the door handle, a sob made her turn. Her eyes widened when she saw Mrs. Little, one of the local shopkeepers, standing on the street with her young daughter Sharlene at her side, a man in a tailored coat and lace at the wrists the object of her pleas.

"We have no money to travel to my sister's," the woman was saying. "How're we supposed to get there?"

"I'm sorry," the man replied. "There's nothing I can do." Then he turned and went back into the shop.

Emma watched this in shock. The poor woman's husband had died not six months earlier, and together they had run the local bakery. Why was this other man inside her shop and Mrs. Little outside?

"Mrs. Little?" Emma said as she hurried to the distraught woman. "What has happened?"

The woman worried a kerchief in her fingers and her face lined with tears. "Oh, Emma, since Paul passed, I've struggled to pay the rent. I didn't know he'd taken out loans, and he'd already spent every pence we had in savings."

Emma nodded. It was well-known that Mr. Little had a problem with drinking and gambling, a seemingly common issue of many if the people's books were any indication. Emma had tried to warn Mrs. Little, but what could she do? Her husband had complete control over their finances, and the woman could do nothing to keep him from squandering away everything they had.

Glancing down at Sharlene, a child of no older than seven, Emma could not help but lament for them both. Sharlene wiped her nose on the sleeve of her coat, sniffling as tears ran rivers down her cheeks.

"I overheard you say you are trying to get to your sister's," Emma said.

"Yes. Mary lives near Cambridge, but we have no money to get there. We're much too far away to walk, but I suppose if we must…" She glanced down at her daughter and wiped away her tears with a kerchief.

"But then to have enough for food, as well? We'll be on the road for weeks, and I've only a few shillings left to my name. Mr. Charleton says Paul left so much debt that even taking the shop can't cover it. He's agreed to accept just the shop, but now there's nothing left to take care of us. I've no idea what we're going to do." She began to sob into her kerchief, and Emma could do nothing but watch as the woman grieved.

And yet...She squeezed the small purse in her pocket. She had a general idea of the cost of a carriage to Cambridge, for she had seen the costs in a recent ledger entry. The money in her purse would be enough to not only pay for a ticket there, but it would be enough for food and lodging along the way.

"Take this," she said as she placed the entirety of her savings into the hands of Mrs. Little. "May you find a new start that is better than what you leave here."

"Oh, Emma," the woman said as she attempted to return the purse. "I cannot. I know we're all suffering in these hard times."

"No, you must take it. You are my friend, and I will not see you or little Sharlene here," she patted the girl on the head, "suffer."

Mrs. Little sniffled. "One day, if I'm able, I'll find a way to repay you."

Emma smiled. "You cannot repay a gift."

This brought on a new bout of tears, and the woman pulled Emma in for a tight embrace. "I don't know how I'll ever thank you, but I pray that good fortune falls upon you." She turned to her young daughter. "Come, Sharlene, we are going to see your Auntie Arabella." Then she gave Emma a wide smile, tears still glinting in her eyes. "Thank you again, Emma."

"Safe travels," Emma replied, and she smiled as the pair walked away. She truly did hope better days would come to Mrs. Little and her child, for the woman deserved such happiness. To have gone through the life she had and remain the same kind woman she had always been was an accomplishment, and Emma said a silent prayer of a good life for them both.

Before Emma made her way back to her father's office, she stopped once more before the window of the dressmaker's shop. Her dream of a new dress would have to wait for now.

She would begin saving anew, and in time she would have enough to make such a purchase, but for now, that money was going to better use. The dresses she owned were still serviceable for the time being, and the purchase of the new dress would have been superfluous, anyway. More important things existed in the world, that much was certain.

The shop door opened, and two women stepped out, followed by a man in livery carrying wrapped packages. One of the women assessed Emma before crinkling her nose at her, as if encountering an unpleasant odor.

Emma offered the woman a smile despite the disgusted look she received, but it was met with a derisive glare before the two women walked past her as if she were a stray dog in the street. It was not the first time women of the *ton* had treated her in such a manner; therefore, Emma ignored their looks and returned her gaze to the window. Seeing her reflection, she sighed at what she saw, for she could never compare to the ladies who frequented such a shop. Yet, this was her life, and only she could do something about it. Therefore, she returned to the office, determined to complete the tasks required of her for what remaining clients her father had. That was all she could do for the moment.

Chapter Two

Lucas Redstone, Duke of Rainierd, was not one for patience. He believed that a person, more specifically a servant, should be instructed once and no more, for his time was much more precious than that of those around him. If it were not for him, those in his employ would not have an income and therefore would have no means for which to take care of themselves.

Apparently, that lesson had fallen on deaf ears as Louise, one of the upstairs maids who had been a member of his staff for many years, stood before him in his study. Her lip trembled, and the thought of the woman falling into tears only fueled his anger, for the sight of a woman weeping was a thing for which he had even less tolerance.

"Your Grace," the maid whispered, "I beg your forgiveness. I lost track of time—"

Lucas raised a hand, and the woman halted her excuse. "Do you wish to find employment elsewhere?" he asked, and the woman shook her head. "Then perhaps you can explain to me why I had to be pulled from my important work in order to deal with the fact that you began work late this morning. The others rose long before the sun, and yet you preferred to lay abed while they work?" He drew in a lungful of air and held it in an attempt to keep his temper as he glanced at the beautiful paintings and fine rugs from India. Did this servant somehow believe herself better than he?

"I apologize, Your Grace," Louise said with a whimper. "I was awake until well past three helping to clean the ballroom and returned to my quarters much later than I'm accustomed.

9

It won't happen again, I promise!"

Then the inevitable tear escaped her eye as her lip trembling increased, and Lucas shook his head as his anger turned to sorrow. Had he not told Mrs. Flossum, the head housekeeper, just this morning how impressed he had been with how the ballroom sparkled? It had been Mrs. Flossum who had come to him when Louise had not reported to her duties on time, a request he had made of her years earlier in order to keep the staff free of lazy servants. Now, Louise stood before him, exhaustion written on her face, and he was left to reprimand her after her hard work. Suddenly, the idea appalled him.

Yet, he was a duke, and any mercy shown could be taken as weakness, and that was the least tolerant thing he could endure. Therefore, he had to show strength in order to gain the respect of those on whom he placed such demands. If he were to show this servant mercy, she might tell the other servants, and then others might get it into their heads to slack in their own duties. No, he needed to be firm in every decision he made, and if it meant using one maid as an example, there was little he could do about it.

"You will retain your position in this house," he said, ignoring her whispers of gratitude. "But I will dock your pay this week. In time, you will learn to act with responsibility, or you will be released from your position to make way for someone who will not take it for granted."

"Yes, Your Grace," she said with a curtsy, and as she lowered her head in reverence, he saw the streaks of silver in her otherwise dark hair. He remembered a time when her hair was all black, although that had been some years ago. Sometimes, as a young boy, he would follow Louise as she performed her duties, the woman happy to speak with him and share tales in order to amuse him. Only a chambermaid at the time, she had moved up to her current position through hard work and diligence. As she raised her head, guilt ran through him and he had to turn his back to her to keep from showing any emotion. Even if she had been kind to him as a child, she was still his servant, and therefore had to be kept at a distance.

"Off with you, then," he said. "Continue your work."

When the woman was gone, he heaved a sigh, glad that task was completed. As he left the study and made his way to the office that had once belonged to his father, other servants moved out of his way, pressing their backs against the wall and looking down at the floor as he passed. He did not blame them; how many times had he lost his temper and shouted at one or another?

The office had not changed since the passing of his father with its fall oak bookcases, dark oak furniture with red velvet cushions, and a large window that looked over the lush gardens to the back of Bonehedge Estates. His grandfather, the First Duke of Rainierd, had found a bone in one of the hedges when he and the architect he had enlisted were looking at the property; thus, the name. Now it seemed dissatisfying, but changing it after this long was illogical, so it would remain as such.

The gardens were as magnificent as the house itself with its pathways that wound through flowerbeds and trimmed bushes. If only he had time to spend enjoying it, but at least he had a pleasant view when he needed a break from the mountain of work he had.

He had assumed the title from his father at the age of seventeen and had been busy learning the trade since. Now, at the age of five and twenty, and with his mother away at her estate in Scotland, he finally felt he understood his responsibilities. Because he had spent so long concentrating on becoming a duke as great as his father had been, he and his mother had not seen each other in a few years, and he had taken little time to write her any letters.

"Your Grace?"

Lucas turned to find his butler at the door, a silver tray in his hand. "Yes, Goodard? What is it?"

"A letter has arrived for you," the older man said as he presented the tray to Lucas.

"It is from Albert," Lucas said after opening the document and looking at the closing. His eyes read over the letter. "What is this?" he asked, unable to believe what he was reading. His breathing became harsh as his temper rose. "How dare he!"

"Your Grace?" Goodard asked in alarm.

"I believe Albert is cheating me!" he shouted. "In fact, I know he is."

11

"Shall I send word that you require his presence?" Goodard asked, his posture as rigid as his voice. He always did take anything that happened to Lucas as if it were an affront to himself.

Lucas thought for a moment. "No, that will not be necessary," he replied finally. "My ledgers will be arriving today, and I will have too much to do to deal with him."

Goodard offered him a smile. "Very well, Your Grace." He paused. "There is another matter to discuss."

Lucas sighed. Of course there was. "What is it?"

"While I was in the village this morning, I had the honor of speaking with Lady Paulette Mathers. She spoke highly of your party last evening and asked that I relay what a splendid time she had."

Lucas snorted. "She ate and drank enough," he said with disgust as he thought on the eldest daughter of Baron Mathers. "I am certain she has nothing about which to complain. Any other messages?"

The old man smiled, a twinkle in his eye. "Lady Paulette also said she looks forward to coming to dinner this Friday. Have you found a woman for your arm?"

If any other man had spoken to Lucas in such a manner, he would have thrown him out on his ear. What business was it of a servant to ask such a question? Goodard had been a friend for years, despite his position. If it had not been for his support, Lucas was uncertain if he would have remained as sane as he was.

Then guilt hit him. Why had he been so harsh with Louise, a woman who had been in his household as long as Goodard, but gave Goodard certain allowances? Well, it did not matter; he was the duke and could treat any servant any way he chose.

Ignoring the thought, he said, "Lady Paulette is a beautiful woman, but she seems as dense as the sheep in the fields."

"Most women are, Your Grace," Goodard replied with a light chuckle. "And, indeed, she is beautiful, which would make her a more than suitable bride. As long as you are happy in her presence, that is what matters."

Lucas considered the old man's words. Lady Paulette did have a beauty about her, but even so, he felt nothing for her. How could he?

The woman had to be one of the most boring women he had ever encountered, her conversational topics revolving around what events were taking place and who would be attending. Any topics of any substance were pushed aside almost immediately. Lucas knew he would have to marry one day, but that day was not today, and especially not to one such as Lady Paulette.

"Marriage is a long way away," Lucas replied. "Leave me, Goodard. I have much to consider." The butler bowed and left him alone.

Lucas returned to the letter and his anger returned. It was not only the possibility of being cheated that made his ire grow but his inability to keep his own books. Try as he might, numbers confused him and therefore, he had been forced to keep the bookkeeper his father had used before his death.

Sitting back in his chair, his mind wandered to Lady Paulette once again. He supposed it was time he found himself a wife, yet no woman had caught his eye nor piqued his curiosity. Women of the *ton* tended to be shallow in thought and held little interest for him, but there had to be a woman out there who would be a compatible addition to his household.

Sighing, he picked up the letter and read it again. He had other concerns at the moment much more pressing than concerning himself with a bride he had yet to meet.

***

Numbers might have been a constant annoyance to Lucas, but as he ran his finger down the columns, he saw that something was terribly wrong. According to the sums, he was losing nearly two hundred pounds a month, and that did not sit well with him. The loss of even the smallest amount was concerning, but the amount he was seeing? Outrageous! Lucas rubbed his temples. First, it seemed Albert had been cheating him, and now, another man, a marquess no less, had been doing the same!

"These numbers are wrong," he said, looking up from the ledgers and glaring at the man standing before him. "Your name again?"

"Stephen, Your Grace," he said with a bow of his head. The man was older, and Lucas thought he knew him from somewhere, but he could not place where. "I do believe they're correct, Your Grace."

Lucas slammed his fist on the table, his voice bellowing, "Do not tell me that the mistake lies with my own recordkeeping!" He rose from the desk, and the man trembled. "Did you go over these numbers?"

"I did, Your Grace," the man croaked. "Double and treble checked them."

"Why has Mr. Barrington passed off my work to you?" Lucas asked, reaching across the desk to grab the second ledger from the man's hand. "Does he have more important clients than me?" He slammed the ledger on top of the other, stood, and walked around the desk. "Answer me! Does he believe he is better than me?"

"N-no, Your Grace," Stephen stammered. "No one would upset the Duke of Storms!" He slammed his jaw closed and his eyes flew open wide.

"What was that?" Lucas asked, peering into the man's eyes. "The Duke of Storms, is it?"

"Beggin' your forgiveness, Your Grace," he whispered. The hand holding his hat in front of him trembled. "It was a slip of the tongue."

Lucas narrowed his eyes. "And it could be a costly one," he said, seething. He was well aware that the moniker had been assigned to him because of his temper, and he loathed it. Some of the stories told about him were true while others were not, but he had yet to hear them from someone who did not know him directly. "What have you heard about me?"

Stephen swallowed hard. "N-nothing, Your Grace."

Lucas took a step closer. "Do not lie. Tell me what you have heard."

The hesitation disappeared and the man's voice came clear and quick. "That you've been known to call down lightning from the sky. They say there's thunder in your footsteps that sends the animals of the forest running."

Although anger still boiled in Lucas, he could not help but laugh. "Call down lightning?" he asked incredulously. "As though I am a deity of the Greeks of ancient times?"

The man nodded. "Yes, Your Grace. That exactly."

Lucas shook his head. "The foolery of the *ton* runs deep," he murmured.

"Not the *ton*," Stephen said. "In fact, from the youngest of children to farmers, everyone knows about..." His voice trailed off and he cringed, as if he expected Lucas to strike him down where he stood.

Lucas turned and picked up the ledgers. "Tell me," he growled, "what do you see wrong with the column on the last page?"

Stephen took the ledger with a shaky hand and flipped through to the last page containing writing. He scanned over it for a moment before looking up and replying, "Nothing, Your Grace. It's accurate."

Lucas scrunched his brow. "Are you certain?" he asked. The book was upside down.

"Yes, Your Grace," Stephen replied. "All is in order. In fact—"

With a growl, Lucas grabbed the book. He now knew who this man was, why he was so familiar. "You are old Stephen the Drunk. You cannot read or write, can you?"

In the distance, thunder rumbled as the first spits of rain tapped against the window behind him. The man did not need to answer as memories flooded Lucas's mind. When he was ten, he remembered the town drunk, a man who stumbled out of a public house and bumped into Lucas. He had apologized and then promptly fell over on his face, apparently succumbed to the drink. And now, this same man was viewing his personal records? The idea was a direct insult to his station!

"Your Grace, if you'd allow me to—"

The wind began to howl outside the window, and rain now pounded on the panes.

"Quiet!" Lucas said. The rumors were false, and yet Lucas felt he could control the storm outside. What a pity he could not control the one within. How he wished he could send lightning down and burn the man in front of him from his sight! "Is Mr. Barrington in his office today?"

"N-no, Your Grace," Stephen whispered. "He's gone to London. But his daughter's there."

"His daughter?"

"Y-yes, M-Miss Emma," the man stammered but then gave Lucas a toothy grin. "Such a kind woman, Miss Emma. One who is both charitable and—"

"I did not ask after her character," Lucas snapped as he returned to his desk. He took a seat and pulled the ledger to him. "Is his daughter minding the office?"

Stephen's grin widened. "More than that, Your Grace. She's in charge of everything!"

The realization of what had happened came crashing in on Lucas. With her father away, the woman thought she was capable enough to run his business. It explained why the numbers were off and why the fool in front of him had been tasked to deliver the ledgers.

"The madness of people never ceases to amaze me," he mumbled. "It is no wonder so many of the *ton* are finding themselves without a home." He looked up at the old man again. "You may leave, but give this Miss Emma a message from me."

"Yes, of course," the man said with eagerness. "What'll I tell her?"

"Tell her that the Duke of Storms is not happy."

Chapter Three

Thunder rumbled as Emma looked out onto the empty street. Streams of water rushed along the ruts in the mud, dark clouds blocking out the sun that would have been on the western horizon. If only she could enjoy the pinks and oranges of the sunset.

"Miss Emma?"

Emma jumped. She had not heard Stephen return. She took one last look at the downpour and sighed. "How did it—" She stopped when she saw the look of the older man.

"I'm sorry," he said, sniffling. "If he means to hang anyone, let it be me. It was my big mouth and not being able to read that made him angry." He pulled out a dirty kerchief and wiped his nose. "He's right. I'm nothing but an old drunk."

Emma was surprised at the bloodshot eyes and the sadness on Stephen's face. "You might have been a drunk before, but you are now my friend. You will be a good businessman if I have anything to say about it." This made the old man's face lighten. "And I, for one, am proud of how far you have come in the past year."

"Thank you, Miss Emma," he said with another sniff. "It's because of you and your father, you know. You've been so good to me. No one else would talk to me, but you did."

She smiled, for his words were true. For years, she had seen the old drunk around town, oftentimes mumbling to himself and acting the fool. Emma had reached out to him, nonetheless. She needed help in the office, she had told him, but he had to promise to quit his drinking. Although he was old and illiterate, he had made good on his promise and became more than an assistant but a dear friend, as well.

Stephen grasped his hat in his fists. "Without a friend like you, I don't think I'd make it."

"I feel the same, my friend," she replied with a warm smile. "And no, you will not be hanged. No one will. I will speak to the duke myself when he arrives."

Thunder boomed, much closer this time. Was it an omen of things to come? She shook her head. What nonsense! She was never one for believing in omens or other superstitions, and she would not begin now.

Walking over to Stephen, she straightened the collar of his coat. It was as old and tattered as he, but it was clean. They had fallen on hard times, much like most in the village, and it would take an abundant amount of luck to climb from the depths in which they found themselves. "Now, I would like you to return home and rest for the evening. Take pride in knowing you have done nothing wrong."

"Thank you, Miss," he said, sniffling as she pulled him in for a light embrace. "I'll be here bright and early in the morning."

She walked him to the door. "See that you are," she said with feigned fierceness. "Having a duke angry with us does not change the fact we have work to do."

He gave her one of his wide grins and then he was gone.

As she went to close the door, a familiar carriage trumbled by. The daughter of a butcher, Susan Thompson had been a friend before she married a wealthy man and had become Mrs. Rumsfeld. Now that she was of the gentry, the woman had no time for the likes of Emma, or anyone else of the working class.

As Emma thought on her old friend, she realized that all of her friends were now married, many with children of their own. Emma, on the other hand, had remained unattached, not even courted by a man, and instead had stayed to help her father with his business.

With the business now in decline, she found she had no time for parties or gatherings. Nor friends, for that matter. One by one, they went on with their lives while she continued in hers. And so the wheel turned.

It was not as if she did not enjoy helping her father, for she did.

She could not stop the dreams of meeting a kind man, one who would love her and, even more, understand her. For the burden she carried was great, one of which no one but Stephen was aware. To share a burden with a friend was not the same as sharing with a husband, or so she imagined. A man to hold her, to cherish her, and to allow her to share that which was on her heart.

The thunder rattled the panes of the window, a deep booming that made Emma start. Then the door opened, and a man with long, dark hair entered the office. Although she had only seen him once in her life, his presence made her fearful, for it was none other than the Duke of Storms.

"You are Miss Barrington, I presume?" he said in a rough, yet sophisticated voice as he glared down at her with his strong blue eyes. Although he was intimidating with his broad shoulders and thick chest, she could not help but notice he had a handsomeness about him with his defined jaw and perfect cheekbones. "Are you deaf?" he demanded.

"No," Emma replied as she lowered herself into an unpracticed curtsy. She had few occasions to use such diffidence; she would have to practice if she was made to interact more with clients of this man's station, something for which she had not planned. "Forgive me, Your Grace. It is an honor to have you in our office."

He gave a quick glance around the room and crinkled his nose. "My stables are better decorated," he said.

She felt a surge of anger begin to rise in her. That is, until he turned and their eyes met. Perhaps the weather was making her ill, for her vision swam for several moments. It was strange, somehow, for his eyes reminded her of a roiling sea, bold and beautiful in their majesty.

"But I am not here to discuss your office. I assume you know why I am here."

"Yes," she replied, focusing her thoughts on the matter at hand. "If you would give me a moment to explain—"

"No!" he barked, and the wind pelted the rain against the window creating an eerie clamor. Or was it perhaps simply the duke's presence that produced such a sound? "You will listen. I have been gracious enough to allow your father to attend to my books."

He closed his eyes and sighed before walking over to a small painting that hung on the wall. He reached up and traced along its frame. "And what do I receive in return? A woman?"

Emma made no comment. What could she say? Most men thought the same whenever they were forced to meet with a woman for business. Why would this man be any different? As he turned, she thought of the rumors she had heard about the Duke of Storms. Would he call down the lightning to strike her? He certainly appeared as though he could.

"A woman," he repeated, harsher this time. "What does a woman know of bookkeeping? Or of business, for that matter? Tell me the answer to this riddle, for it eludes me."

Emma nodded, swallowing the retort that rose inside her. Although her fear was great, she replied, "Since I was a child, my father taught me his business. I have been under his tutelage for more than a dozen years, and I know what needs to be done as well as he."

The duke snorted. "That is why you allow a drunk to assist you?" he demanded.

"Stephen is no drunk," she snapped back. How dare this man call attention to a man who had worked so hard to strip away his past! "Stephen has stopped his foolery. Besides, he does not attend to the books; he only delivers them. That does not take more than the ability to carry something from one place to another."

She halted, realizing how forceful her voice had become. "I am sorry for speaking so harshly. It is the storm; it keeps me on edge." She glanced at the window and returned her gaze to the duke. His coat was the color of his eyes, and she noticed the way his muscles pushed at the sleeves as he straightened his cravat.

"Do not do it again," he said. "But that is irrelevant at the moment. My books are off, and I will not stand for slovenly work."

Emma was taken aback. How dare this man accuse her of poorly executed work! "I assure you," she replied, doing everything she could to keep her tone even, "they were completed properly."

"Your father did the work himself, then?"

"No," she said, pulling herself up straighter. "I completed the work."

For a moment, he only stared at her, but then he pulled his head back and barked a loud laugh. "Yes, I can see the problem now." He walked over and stood not a hand's length away, and Emma found her heart pounding against her chest with a wildness that made breathing difficult. "A woman cannot conduct business, nor can she keep books for such occasions."

Emma held her tongue but with difficulty. It was such a challenge that she had to bite her tongue to keep back the retort that threatened to explode from her lips.

"When will your father return?"

"In four days," Emma replied. "That is, if his meetings in London go as planned."

He nodded. "Very well. In four days send your father to Bonehedge Estates. He has until the clock strikes ten to appear. If he does not..." Without finishing his threat, he turned and walked out the door, slamming it behind him.

Worry coursed through Emma as she ran to the door and opened it. "Your Grace!" she called out into the rain, "and if he is unable to arrive on time?"

The duke stopped and turned to glare at her, the rain streaming off the rim of his hat. "Then I will find someone who will." He turned back around and disappeared into the night.

Emma returned to the room just as the last light of the setting sun disappeared. Dark shadows moved around her as she sat down in the chair belonging to her father, but she made no effort to light a candle. She gave a heavy sigh. Regardless of the man's threats, her father would not arrive at the appointed time. Losing another client, especially one of the caliber of the duke, would more than likely be what drove them into the streets.

Chapter Four

The knots in Emma's stomach began to tighten as the clock struck eight. Two hours remained before the duke would cancel his account, and she had only one course of action that could put a stop to it. She took a deep breath and glanced over at Stephen, who stood with his hands clasped before him.

"Miss Emma," he pleaded, "there must be another way."

She shook her head sadly. "I do not believe there is," she replied with a sigh. "I must do it myself."

"Surely if you tell him the truth? Perhaps he will understand."

"You and I both know that is not possible," Emma replied. Although the thought of lying was unsettling, she had no choice when it came to her father. Many reasons for her deception existed, but if the truth was exposed, all their clients would flee. She sighed again. "I suppose I should go."

"Very well," Stephen replied. "I'll wait here until you return. Are you sure you don't want me to escort you? I'm afraid to have you walking alone at night."

Emma opened the door and turned to give the man an appreciative smile. "That will not be necessary," she said as she took a step out the door only to run straight into the landlord of the property, one Lord Gordon Miggs. He might have been a baron, but Emma found him to be more abhorrent than even the duke. Where the duke was quick to anger, this man held lust in his eyes at any woman under the age of thirty; married or unmarried mattered not to him.

He ran his fingers through what was left of his silver hair. "Ah, Miss Emma," he said in that oily tone she despised. "I have been meaning to speak to you."

"My lord," she replied with a quick curtsy, hating to show any form of diffidence to him. "If it is concerning the rent—"

Lord Miggs raised a hand, and Emma went quiet. "Let us get out of this night air," he said as he took a step forward, forcing her through the door without laying a single finger on her. When he noticed Stephen, he said, "Leave us."

Stephen looked at Emma, who gave him a quick nod. As soon as the man stepped through the door, the baron slammed the door closed, turned around and studied Emma, his hands clasped behind his back. The buttons on his black coat strained to keep his large stomach enclosed in it, as did those on his crisp, white shirt, yet it was the man's dark eyes that had always bothered Emma, for they held a hunger in them that left her feeling somehow soiled.

"The rent is late," he said. "You do realize that I do not run a charity here."

"Yes, my lord," Emma replied. "Times have been difficult, and it is not because I do not care…" Her heart froze as the baron took a step forward and ran the back of his hand down her cheek. The caress brought about revulsion and made her wish to run away, but she held her ground. She could not allow this man to make her feel less than she was.

He licked his lips. "Such a beautiful creature," he whispered. "I know you care, for you are a good woman."

Unsure as to what to do, Emma offered him a forced smile. "I-I appreciate you saying so, my lord."

"To be honest, I thought you were, perhaps, taking advantage of my good nature, but then I thought, no, not Emma." He ran his hands over the bare skin of her arms.

She swallowed hard. "Thank you, my lord," she said, attempting to keep her dinner from rising. "If I could have only another week, I would be most appreciative. Tonight, I am leaving to settle an account, and I shall have the money for the rent when it is completed."

"For both months?"

Emma looked down at the floor. She had not considered he would ask for the current month, as well.

"Ah, I see." He took her hands in his, and she forced herself to look up at him, though she continued to keep herself from sicking up at the way his eyes devoured her. "Well, I am sure you know that the rising costs of maintaining properties such as yours have forced my hand."

"W-what do you mean?"

"I am afraid to say that I will have to raise your rent beginning next month."

Emma's heart fell to the floor. "I cannot pay more," she said with shock. "I beg of you, give me time!"

He narrowed his eyes at her and rubbed his chin. "If it were anyone else, I would say no." He tightened his grip on her hands. "However, this matter must be discussed further. Is that fair?"

Emma felt a sense of relief wash over her and she nodded. "Yes. And thank you." His offer to discuss the matter was gracious. She had seen what had happened to Mrs. Little and her daughter; they were not given any chance at all.

"Then, be at my house by six p.m. tomorrow to discuss your rent and perhaps come to a solution." He looked her up and down. "Be sure to dress, for we will dine together, as well."

His wife had died four years earlier, and rumors of his roguish ways were rampant throughout the village. Emma feared she knew what the baron wanted as payment, but what choice did she have?

"I will be there at six," she replied, although hearing the words aloud made her cringe. "I am late for an appointment, so I must leave."

Much to her relief, he released her hands. "Very good. I look forward to it." He walked to the door but paused. "Oh, and if you do decide to change your mind, just understand that I will be very upset." Before she could respond, he opened the door and closed it behind him.

A moment later, Stephen returned. "Are you all right, Miss Emma?" he asked, concern etched on his face.

"I am," Emma replied, though she could not help but worry that she might have made an unwise decision in meeting with the baron for dinner.

It was too late to back out now. Furthermore, if she did not appease the duke tonight, it would not matter, anyway. "Come. We must be off. We do not want to be late."

Stephen's eyes widened. "You want me to join you?"

"Yes," she replied. "Do not leave me."

The thought of being alone after what had just happened and what she had to face did not sit well with her. Therefore, with her friend by her side, the two left the office, the future as uncertain as ever.

***

The estate on which the duke lived was nearly an hour's walk from the village, and without the benefit of a full moon to guide her steps, Emma was thankful for the company of Stephen. Her mind turned over the plan for this evening and how she would present her story to the duke.

"Don't you worry, Miss Emma," Stephen said from beside her. "You'll be fine; I just know it."

"How did you know I was concerned?" she asked. She had thought she had done an adequate job of hiding her worries. "Do you have the ability to read my thoughts?"

Stephen laughed. "Oh, no, Miss," he said as the large home came into view. "You mumble sometimes when you're thinking is all. Gives you away every time."

Emma could not help but laugh. "I will be certain not to do that again."

With each step, the house appeared larger, and Emma's worry increased. When they finally came up the marble steps that led to the front door, she thought the air around her had disappeared. It took several moments to calm herself before she reached up and knocked on the door.

"You are very brave," Stephen murmured. "You don't have nothing to worry about. Just remain strong."

She placed a hand on his arm. "Thank you for saying so."

Stephen blushed, but his smile beamed greater than the half-moon that had led them down the road. "It's only the truth."

The door opened, and a man Emma presumed to be the butler stood at the entrance. "Please," he said as he moved aside and extended his hand to indicate they should enter.

Emma looked around the foyer, her eyes wide. Dark stained oak ran along the walls and floor. A carpet longer than any she had ever seen ran the length and breadth of the room that could have held not only her office but the flat above it, as well. The chandelier held more candles than she had ever encountered lit in one place.

"This way, please," the old butler said with a kind smile that somehow surprised her. What she expected, she did not know, but kindness had not been on the list, even if the man was a servant. The smile made her straighten her back as she followed the butler down the hallway. She would succeed in keeping the account of the duke if it was the last thing she did!

Although the house was large and the items luxurious, a coldness seeped into her bones, and her temporary burst of courage began to wane. Every piece of furniture and décor had its place, but the house lacked a sense of home.

When they reached a set of tall double-doors, the butler turned to Stephen and said, "If you will have a seat." He indicated a pair of high-back chairs covered in red velvet sitting just outside the doors.

Stephen gave her a concerned look, but Emma nodded. With reluctance, he took a seat, clearly unhappy that Emma was to enter the room alone.

"The duke is waiting," the butler said with a slight nod of his head. He opened the door and announced, "Miss Emma Barrington, Your Grace." Then he gave a deep bow, moved aside, and extended his hand again to indicate she was to enter the room.

The duke stood beside an unlit fireplace, his back to her. Emma worried at her bottom lip as he raised his arm and swept it toward the door. The butler bowed his head and left the two of them alone, closing the door behind him.

The room had tall bookcases built into two of the walls, filled with what had to be every book in existence. A single sofa sat across from two wingback chairs, a low coffee table between them. Above the fireplace was the painting of a family — a man, woman, and a young boy of perhaps ten — the duke's family, she assumed.

The seconds stretched as she waited, and just before she decided to speak, the duke turned, his face solemn and his eyes stern. "Your father?"

"I apologize, Your Grace," she said with a quick curtsy. "He is unable to attend."

The duke gave a nod. He studied her for a moment and then let out a maniacal laugh that made her shiver. "Oh, how my patience has run thin," he said when the strange laugh was gone. In two quick steps, he was before her, glaring down at her like some insect invading his space. "I have been kind enough to you and your father," he said in a low tone that was worse than the laughter he had displayed. "Our relationship is terminated. Now, leave."

Tears filled Emma's eyes before she could stop them. She knew this would be his reaction, had even readied herself for it, yet she responded with tears? She was stronger than this. "Your Grace, please," she whispered, reaching deep inside herself for the strength she needed. "If you would allow me a moment to explain. I received word from my father that his departure from London has been postponed. If you would allow me to go over your books with you, I can—"

The duke curled his lip. "I will not have a woman attempt to explain business matters to me," he said. "Leave at once. I will not ask again."

Accepting defeat, Emma turned. She would not give this man the privilege of seeing her cry. She left the room, and just as the door closed behind her, the tears fell in great streams. She had failed. They would lose the business as well as the office and the small room above where she lived. She was nearly a spinster with no one to love, with only an old baron who lusted after her to whom she could turn.

Bowing her head in shame and defeat, an image of her father came to mind. He had never given up at any time in his life, so why would she? Had she not said on more than one occasion that she could do as well as he? Had her father not said as much himself?

Her composure returned, she placed her hand on the handle to the door she had just exited. duke or not, she would have her say. The business was already lost, and although the Duke of Storms may call down lightning, he was still just a man. And with that thought, she pushed the door open and walked back inside.

Chapter Five

As the door slammed closed, Lucas released a heavy sigh as he tried to understand an unusual feeling inside him. Guilt. His temper had exploded with Miss Barrington, yet that was nothing new. He was prone to outbursts, he was strong enough to admit as much, and this had been minor compared to the explosions he had forced others to endure. Then what brought about this guilt that now hung over him?

It had to be the tears that had brimmed the woman's eyes. Not the fact she was near weeping, for more than one maid had wept during one of his tongue-lashings. What he saw was a woman who had the strength to keep the tears from falling, which was a rare sight, indeed.

She was beautiful, far more than any woman he had ever seen; even in her tattered dress and bonnet, she could not hide that fact. Yet, that beauty was not confined to that which was seen; inside was a strength the woman could control. It was strange to see someone with the ability to take hold of her emotions with little struggle. How he wished he could do the same with his temper.

Now, with her gone, he wondered if perhaps he should have listened to what she had to say. Although his father had taught him women knew nothing of business — or anything beyond dresses and planning dinner parties, for that matter — perhaps this woman was different.

He shook his head. The beauty of this woman had to be muddling his thinking. All women were the same, and to think that, somehow, she was not like the others was foolishness on his part.

What he had done was for the best, but now he had to search for a new bookkeeper. That would be a daunting task, for Mr. Barrington had been the only person to keep his books for him. Well, he had several men he knew who used such services; he would query them.

As he moved to return to his desk, the door opened, and he was shocked when he turned and saw Miss Barrington storm back into the room.

"I do not care if you call down lightning to strike me!" she shouted, slamming the door shut behind her. "Nor do I care if you are a duke. Have me beheaded or hanged, ruined and chastised, whatever it is you do to those who cross you, but I have nothing more to lose, so I will have my say!"

Lucas stared at the woman. He had never seen such fire — such passion — from any woman. Even few men displayed this much anger with such poise. Her voice was strong, her eyes fierce, and her features determined. And in all of that, he had a newfound respect for her.

"Very well," he replied, pulling his chair to the desk as he sat. He did not offer a chair, nor would he; a line had to be drawn somewhere. "Tell me what you must. Amuse me."

Miss Barrington jutted out her chin and walked over to stand in front of his desk, each step steady, yet somehow graceful. She stood with her head held high, her hands at her side rather than wringing in front of her as so many who stood in her place in the past had done.

Was it strange he found himself resisting the urge to walk around the desk and take her in his arms?

"I have assisted my father for years," she said. She spoke rather well for a woman of the working class. "In that time, we have made very few errors, I assure you. When it came to your books, my father always triple checked, for he valued your custom."

"Then why are there mistakes now?" he asked, his eyebrows raising, as was his voice. His amusement could only last so long.

"I do not know," she replied, her voice still as firm as when she entered the room. "I can assure you that it is not my fault."

"Do you mean to say," he said, leaning forward and placing hands on the desk, "that this is somehow a fault of mine?" He narrowed his eyes at her. "And I would answer with care, if I were you."

"If it is not mine," she said, matching his stare, "then the fault lies with someone else. Do you allow others to handle your receipts or record keeping?"

He grinned at her reply. The woman did have a strong wit.

"Now," she continued before he could reply to her question, "you have a choice in this matter."

"Do I?" he asked with a light chuckle. "Tell me, Spinster, what choice do I have?" He regretted the use of spinster as soon as he saw her wince.

"Allow me to look over your receipts and your ledgers, the ones you keep for yourself. I may find the error there." She sighed. "Or not. It is your choice, Your Grace. I will not allow the blunder to fall on me if I was not the one to commit it." She clasped her hands together in front of her and wrung them, for the first time expressing her worry.

Lucas considered these 'choices' as she called them. She had failed to admit another choice, which was to simply ask her to leave and allow him to engage another bookkeeper. Yet he found he could not do so. What was it she had said when she began this tirade?

"You said you care not for how I might what?" He paused as if to think. "Call down lightning? Is it true what that drunk told me? Is my temper so great that people fear me in such a manner?"

"I do not fear you like the others," she said, her hands returning to her sides, although they grasped her skirts. Then she took a deep breath. "Well, if I am honest, I do a little."

"I would never hurt you," he said and then started. An odd sensation came over him, some sort of emotion he could not name. What he had said seemed to hang in the air, and although he was uncertain what he meant by those words, she seemed to garner understanding from them, for she did not appear confused in any way.

The silence hung over the room like a heavy blanket on a summer's night. He had to say something, or he would be suffocated. "You said there is nothing left to lose. What did you mean?"

She bit at her bottom lip, clearly not realizing how enticing such a subtle movement was. "You see, as times have affected both the rich and the poor, we continually lose clients. Many walked away without means in which to pay us. If we lose your account, we will lose our business as well as our home."

He imagined this woman with no place to live, and the idea pierced his heart. Such a scenario for anyone would be horrible enough, but when he placed her there, he found such a circumstance unfathomable.

"I do not lie in order to garner pity," she said, her voice but a whisper. "My story is true. I must have this chance to review your record keeping. I believe something is amiss, and I have the capabilities to learn the truth."

He sighed as he pushed away from the desk and walked over to stare out the window. He never showed pity to anyone, for inside him the storm always raged. Her words, her simple presence, seemed to calm the waves of anger. He cared nothing for her accounting; his interests lay in her ability to control her own storm, and he was determined to learn how she did it.

"Thank you, Your Grace," Miss Barrington said with a resolved sigh when he did not respond. "I will leave now."

Another odd sensation, as if he had received some fright, rushed through him. It was as if he knew, somewhere deep inside himself, that if she left at that moment, he would regret it for the remainder of his life.

"Wait," he called after her.

She stopped and turned back toward him but did not respond.

He rushed to her and she winced as if expecting a blow from his fist. Another pierce to his heart. "I...will you help me? With my books, of course."

She nodded. "I can have Stephen collect your ledgers at a time which is convenient for you."

Her scent pulled him in — lavender soap if he guessed correctly — and he somehow needed her near him. Sending his books to her office would not allow that. "You may come here," he said. She scrunched her brows, and he feared she would not agree. "I will pay you for your time, of course, and I offer you my carriage as a means of transportation." That provocative worrying of her lip made him want to smile, but he did not.

"I do not know," she said finally. "Would it not be easier for you to send the ledgers to my office?"

"Perhaps," he replied, an idea forming in his mind. "I would like you to teach me." He could sense her slipping away, for she gave him a suspicious look. "I am afraid that organization is not one of my strong suits, and I must admit that mathematics has always been a struggle. You clearly have an ability to do both. Will you help me?" His heart raced. Although what he said was true, why would he tell this woman such intimate details only a few knew about him? And for the first time that he could recall, he was worried someone might tell him no.

"Very well, then," she replied after some thought. "I am unable to come right away. I will be available in two days' time, however."

He gave a silent sigh of relief. "Excellent. I look forward to it."

With a nod, she went to the door, and he hurried to open it for her. "Miss Barrington?" he said as she stepped into the hallway, "I admire your ability to speak on your own behalf."

She smiled at him, and he thought he had never seen anything so lovely in all his life.

"I admire your ability to listen," she said as her smile widened.

When she was gone, he returned to his office. A strangeness came over him, for he laughed. Not in anger, but in some newfound joy. For the first time in many years, the storm inside him lay silent.

Chapter Six

The dress Emma had chosen was well out of fashion — no, it had never been in fashion if truth be told — but it was the finest she owned. White muslin with light-blue lace, it had always been her favorite despite its fraying edges. This one she saved for special occasions, and she knew the baron would appreciate it. She did her best to style her hair, pulling it up in the manner of those of the *ton* and leaving several strands to hang down her cheeks. Her choice in what she wore did not come from any hope of winning the eye of the baron, but rather to keep him happy as she fought to save her father's flailing business.

The carriage Lord Miggs had sent made its way down the muddy streets, and Emma peered out the window. Her mind reviewed the last few days, weeks, and even years. She would be five and twenty soon, growing old without children and, more importantly, a husband. The only men in her life were clients, two of which were of the *ton*. One of those two had a horrible temper and the other was filled with lust. She feared the latter over the former.

Although she had not believed the duke would have struck her for returning after he had sent her away, his temper had her cowering in fear before she was able to rein in on her emotions. It was with relief that she gave him a piece of her mind, though she trembled with each word. By the time she had finished, she was filled with panic. She could do nothing but wonder if she had lost her mind, for she certainly had lost his account. Or so she had thought.

Once they had come to an agreement and she had looked into his eyes, she was shocked to see a calmness that had not been there before. The storm had passed, and she had lived. He then had smiled, bringing about a calmness she had not felt in a long time. The worries over her father, the business, and life were swept away with the gentle breeze of his words that promised to soothe any who would listen.

It had been a shock when he had asked her to teach him. At first, she thought he was mocking her, but his voice had been kind and his eyes pleading. She had felt such a warmth rush through her, a pleasant feeling she had never felt before and would not mind if she felt again.

The duke was handsome, once one was able to look beyond his anger. The question was, would that temper of his remain contained during their lessons, or would he become frustrated and unleash that storm once more?

"Oh, what had I been thinking?" she whispered. Yet, she had no choice in the matter, no more choice than she had in attending this horrid dinner with Lord Miggs this night. No such demands would have been forced upon her father if he had been in attendance! Yet, life was what it was.

As the carriage trumbled along, her mind wandered, and images of she and the duke courting played in her mind. What a wonderful thought! They would walk through the magnificent gardens — she imagined they would be magnificent; she had yet to see them — and he would offer her his arm…

She laughed. A duke courting a spinster from the working class? The chances of a man genuinely calling forth lightning were more likely to happen! She was a woman of better sense than to give herself to flights of fancy, and she pushed aside the images, delectable as they were, and focused on the task at hand.

The carriage came to a stop in front of a house that was not as large as she had expected. Oh, it was certainly much larger than the office and room she occupied at the moment, but from what Lord Miggs had said, his home should have been at least thrice the size of this one.

As she stepped from the carriage, the door of the house opened, and Lord Miggs stood on the stoop, his black coat and breeches pressed to perfection, his cravat tied just so. Unfortunately for him, it did nothing to make him look less slippery.

"Miss Emma," he said as he came down the single step to meet her, "I take it your journey went well."

Emma had to stifle a laugh, for he made it sound as if she had traveled a great distance in order to see him when, in fact, she had been in the carriage less than thirty minutes. "Yes," she replied, lifting her skirts and curtsying. "Thank you for sending the carriage."

The baron nodded to the driver, who dipped his head and returned to the carriage before driving it away. "Dinner will be served soon. I thought that perhaps we would walk the grounds?"

"That would be lovely," Emma lied. The idea of walking with this man made her ill, but she reminded herself of the reason for accepting his invitation. When the baron offered his arm, she rested her hand upon it and they walked around to the back of the house, passing a large oak tree with wide branches that created a wide expanse of shade beneath them as it would be another hour before the sun set below the horizon.

"I am glad the rain has stopped," Emma said in an attempt to bring sound to the otherwise quiet that surrounded them. It helped calm her nerves, even if it was her own voice she heard.

"Indeed" was all the baron replied, and Emma felt a sense of foreboding as they moved further from the house. Did this man mean her harm? But no, that made no sense, for he might lust after her, but he certainly was not evil.

Further down the path they followed, they came upon a creek small enough to jump across if she had been able to lift her skirts high enough. "It is nice to have this so close to the house," the baron said as they walked beside the gentle flow of water. "I did not bring you here to speak of a creek. Nor the weather." He stopped and turned to her, a crooked smile on his face that made her uneasy. "Where is your father?"

The question caught her off-guard, and her mind scurried to find a reasonable answer.

"He has not been seen in nearly a year," he continued. "Has he left you alone?"

"Oh, no, my lord," Emma replied, her heart and mind racing. "He has returned several times, although only for a few days at a time before he is called away again. I am afraid he has been very busy with his London clients."

"And he believes these clients to be of more importance than those already in his care?"

"Not at all," Emma assured him. She searched her mind for any words that would ease the clear concern the man possessed. "The truth of the matter is that he finds them much less agreeable, for they make more demands on him. Rest assured that he prefers local business by far."

Lord Miggs halted beside a bush trimmed to resemble a horse. "You would not lie to me, would you?"

"No, my lord."

Her stomach knotted as he raised his hand and stroked her cheek, part of her wishing to push his hand away, for she found his touch nauseating. It took every ounce of her strength to keep from recoiling. If she were to do so, she would not only lose a client but her home and place of business, as well.

"No," he said in that cloying voice drenched in lust, "I do not think you would." His hand moved down her cheek to her shoulder and then to her arm, lingering there for several moments on her bare skin before he dropped it to his side once more.

She found her breath once more, and she had to stop herself from sighing with relief.

"We must discuss your rent," Lord Miggs said as if the intimate moment had not taken place. "You are delinquent, and I am in the business of making money not losing it. Did you bring your payment as you promised?"

Emma looked down at the ground. She had anticipated the question, but it did not make it any easier to reply. "No, my lord. I am sorry. I am working on accounts at the moment…" She paused when the baron raised an eyebrow. "That is, I am collecting payments for the accounts. My father's assistant does all the work, and I assist him."

The grin the baron gave her made her wonder if he believed her. Rather than discuss his belief or disbelief of the excuses she gave, he said, "Now, what shall I do? Continue to lose money?

Or perhaps I should throw you out into the streets?" He waited as if to assess her response to this suggestion, and she clutched her skirts to keep her features serene. "Perhaps we can come to some sort of agreement? Yes, I believe we can."

"I would like that," Emma said with a relieved sigh. "What can I do?"

"Tomorrow I leave for two weeks. When I return, I will send word for you to come and dine with me again. You must accept, regardless of what you are doing at the time and with whom. Are you willing to do that?"

Emma nodded without thought. That was an easy enough request. A second dinner with him would not be a problem and well worth saving the business.

Lord Miggs smiled that oily smile once more. "Very well, then. You may delay the payment by two more weeks, and I will not even ask for interest."

"Thank you, my lord," Emma replied, doing nothing to hide her relief this time.

"One more thing," he added with a wide grin that held little mirth. "In just over a month's time, the Earl of Bronsley, a dear friend of mine, is hosting a small party. You will join me as my guest." The last was made as a statement and not a request.

Emma considered her options and realized she had none. Therefore, she gave a nod of agreement.

"Good." He offered her his arm again, and they walked back toward the house. "You will find working with me has many benefits." He turned that disconcerting smile back on her once more. "I know I look forward to working with you. I hope you feel the same."

"I do," Emma replied, but doubt crept in like a sudden fog, and she could not shake the feeling of regret that hid in it.

***

The home of Lord Miggs was much larger inside than it had first appeared. The dining room was decorated with light green wallpaper and gilt-framed portraits that looked down upon its guests as a host of servants served a dinner of lamb and stewed tomatoes accompanied by a bottle of red wine.

As luck would have it, the baron had been polite during the meal, and Emma began to wonder if she had misinterpreted his actions by the creek.

Once dinner was completed, they made their way to the parlor. It had deep brown oak walls and a low sculpted ceiling of the same color. The room had a cramped feeling with its dark and heavy furniture of blue velvet; too many pieces for a room of its size. All of it made the foreboding Emma had already been feeling to grow stronger.

Yet, the baron had been polite despite his intimate advances earlier, and he had been speaking without pause for nearly an hour, the wine nearly gone. Emma was ready to leave, but no opportunity presented itself, so she simply sat and listened; though she could not have repeated most of what he had said in all that time.

Smiling, Lord Miggs reached over with the bottle of wine. "A drop more?"

"I cannot," Emma replied, placing her hand over the top of her glass, for she had said so before and he had still poured her more wine. For a moment, Emma thought she saw a bit of anger rise in his features, but it was gone so quickly, she was unsure if she had seen it in the first place. Just in case she had angered him, she added, "The evening has been very pleasant, but tomorrow my schedule is quite busy. It would do me no good to wake in the morning with a piercing headache because I had consumed too much wine the night before."

He let out a small sigh, and panic gripped her. He was angry. Had she ruined a perfectly good evening by declining an innocent offer?

She forced a smile. "Well, now that I consider it, I suppose one more glass of wine cannot hurt."

This made the baron grin, and he quickly refilled her glass. Then he set the bottle on the table beside her. Rather than returning to his own chair, he sat in the place on the couch beside her.

"Why have you not married?" he asked.

She could not help but stare at him in surprise. Not only did she not wish to discuss a subject so close to her, but she also did not wish to discuss it with him! How dare he ask such a question?

"Do you not wish to share with me?"

She could not remain silent; although, what she wished to do was to storm out of the house and leave him to finish off the rest of the wine alone. She could not do that. "I am helping my father," she replied. What she said was true, even if the answer was incomplete. "Of course, many men do not want a woman who has become a spinster."

"They are fools," Lord Miggs said with a snort. "A woman as beautiful as you, spinster or not, should have every man begging for her hand."

"Thank you," Emma replied. His compliments meant nothing, and the lust in his eyes conveyed his intentions. All she wished to do was leave and return to the safety of her small quarters above the office. "One day, perhaps, but for now I am much too busy to consider marriage. Or courting." She hoped her words would express to this man that she had no interest in him. She could not simply say so outright, not when her livelihood rested in his hands.

"We are all busy," he said as he stood. "So much to do and so little time in which to do it." He walked over to the window, his back to her. "The Earl of Bronsley...his party will be magnificent."

"So you said," Emma replied. She covered the curtness by adding, "I do not know the man myself."

"He is a recluse," the baron said. "Yet, he is a dear friend of mine despite that fact." He then turned, and his eyes seemed to look right through her. "You do not regret agreeing to be my guest at the party, do you?"

With her heart in her throat, Emma managed to reply, "No, of course not. It will be an honor to accompany you to the party."

"Indeed," he replied. "It will be an honor. Now, I have kept you much too late, and you must be well-rested for tomorrow."

"I do," she said as relief rushed over her. "The dinner this evening was lovely. Thank you for the invitation."

Lord Miggs smiled. "Come. Let me escort you to the carriage."

Emma followed the baron out of the room and out to the waiting carriage. Stars lit the sky and the night wind was cool. She prayed he would not use his authority as her landlord to his advantage and was surprised when he simply bowed his head to her. What she had expected was him grabbing her and forcing a kiss on her.

"It has been an honor," he said. "I will send word upon my return. All I ask is that you respond immediately."

"I will," she said, surprised by his kind demeanor. In all the years she had known this man, never had she considered him kind. Perhaps he was simply a lonely old man and her fear had been in vain. "I look forward to your return." She clamped her mouth shut. Why would she say such words, such lies?

The smirk the baron wore showed he did not believe her words any more than she did, but he said nothing as she got into the carriage and he closed the door. Before the carriage moved away, he leaned into the window. "I have a feeling we will see much more of one another," he said with that same smile he had used inside that made her stomach churn.

She offered him a smile as the carriage moved away from the house, and then she leaned back into the cushions and closed her eyes. Dinner with a baron and tutoring a duke. She was not certain into what she had gotten herself, but by the end, the business would be saved. And that was all that mattered.

Chapter Seven

Two days later, Emma found herself at the door leading to the office of the duke, and she was regretting her decision to aid him. He was in a meeting, and from the shouting coming from the other side of the door, it was not going well. In fact, the duke was shouting while the other man uttered apologies.

With her arms wrapped around her stomach, Emma considered leaving. She could return to her office and attempt to find new clients. If she sent Stephen around to the various shops and pubs in the village where many of the local men spent an exorbitant amount of time, perhaps he could reach out and convince them that allowing her father to help with their bookkeeping would be of great benefit to them. That her father might not be at the office on many occasions did not matter, as long as they believed it was he who worked with the figures.

The problem was, she had no money to purchase a new coat for him, which he would need in order to complete such a task. Perhaps she could garner the funds in some other way.

She sighed. The plan appeared plausible on the surface, but beneath it all, she knew it was useless. She was in extreme debt, and any money she could procure would be needed to pay the rent, for without the rent, there would be no office, and without an office, there would be no business.

As a matter of fact, the money in the purse she had given Mrs. Little should have gone toward the rent in the first place; buying a dress had been folly and it was highly doubtful she would have gone through with it if she had kept the funds.

"I am no fool!" the duke yelled, startling Emma from her thoughts. "Either you acquire the goods at the agreed-upon price, or we are done! Now, get out of my sight. You make me sick!"

"Yes, Your Grace," the other man said, his voice as shaky as Emma's legs. "I agree to your terms."

A moment later, the door opened and a man with a ring of gray hair on his head hurried out, taking not a single moment to pay any attention to Emma.

Emma worried her lip, took a deep breath, and then entered the room just as the duke moved to exit the room. The first thing she noticed was how hard and rigid his chest was as her body slammed into his. She had instinctively moved her hands up to push him away, but they landed on his arms and she could feel the muscles through his coat. For a moment, time stood still, all sounds except the beating of her heart absent. She looked up into his eyes and recognized the storm that raged within him as the same, if not worse, than what he had shown her on her previous visit.

"Miss Barrington," he said, the shock in his voice overriding the hint of anger that still lingered, "are you all right? You are not hurt, are you?" His voice had a huskiness to it, and he grabbed her waist, for which she was glad. If he had not, she might have fallen over.

Emma attempted to speak, but her voice was stuck in her throat. The feeling of being held by him was overwhelming, and yet pleasant at the same time, and for a moment, she wished to be held a bit longer.

"Miss Barrington?"

With shock, she realized she still had a hold of his arms, and she gasped before taking a step back. "I-I believe so," she whispered, wondering where her senses had gone. "My head...I am all right."

He released her waist, and she found herself wishing his hands would return. Then she shook the fog from her head and composed herself once more. What was she? Some sort of hussy to wish a man to return his hands to her person?

"Please, come in." The duke moved aside to allow Emma to enter the room. After closing the door, he went over to his desk where numerous ledgers and papers were stacked upon it. "I am afraid I have had a hectic morning.

In my father's day, a man's word was binding, much like these documents." He picked up a batch of papers from the desk. "And now? Now, excuses are made!" He slammed the papers down on the desk and turned back to her, his long hair coming loose from its ribbon at the nape of his neck. "They believe I am a fool!"

Emma had no idea how to respond, but she knew she had to calm him. It was not possible to work with someone in such a state, so she summoned her courage and took two steps toward him. "Your Grace, I do not believe you a fool. And you are right; times have changed. From what I see, you have not."

He narrowed his eyes at her. "Is that an accusation?" he asked, his tone sharp. "Or are you mocking me?"

"No, not at all," Emma replied. "What I meant to say was that your ways are noble. Those who do not adhere to noble ways — and there are many — are the fools. You, Your Grace, are not."

He seemed to consider her words, gave a nod, and then a small smile crossed his lips. As if by magic, his eyes calmed and the storm inside him dissipated. "You are a wise woman," he said. Then he turned and indicated the piles of papers on the desk. "I found some documents I had forgotten to send over with my records." He turned back to her. "Not that I made a mistake, mind you."

Emma stifled a giggle. "Of course not," she replied. "May I look over them?"

He nodded and allowed her to move past him. She selected a few and ran her eyes over the papers, calculating and recalling what she had noted in the ledgers she had kept for him.

Then, a peculiar thing happened. Her eyes left the page she was holding and moved to the duke. It appeared he was staring at her, and he wore a crooked grin, one that was not like that of Lord Miggs. No, this man's smile was innocent, much like a child ready to receive a treat or awaiting the compliment of a tutor.

When he realized she had seen him, he cleared his throat and stepped away to the fireplace, which helped Emma immensely, for she was able to return her attention to the pages before her.

"I have seen some errors already," she said, praying he would remain calm. "May I speak frankly with you, Your Grace?"

"Of course," he replied. Then a tiny smile played at the corner of his mouth. "I promise not to strike you down with lightning."

Emma could not help but laugh, and when he smiled at her, she thought the room would spin out of control around her. Feeling her cheeks burn, she continued. "It is not only your organization that is wanting; your penmanship leaves much to be desired. Some of the words are jumbled and the numbers blend into one another."

The duke frowned. "I know how to write and to complete my sums," he said. "I attended the finest schools in England. Where did you attend?"

Emma pursed her lips and forced herself not to respond in kind, although the words hurt more than he could have imagined. "My mother taught me until she died. I did not have the opportunity to attend school, although I wanted to. And of course, higher education is out of the question for one such as myself."

"You mean one of your station?"

She laughed as she moved to another page. "Not only that, but because I am a woman."

He snorted. "A woman with no schooling who sees mistakes…" He paused, his voice amused.

Emma looked up from the paper she was reading. If this was to be how their time together would be, she would leave, even if it meant losing him as a client. She should not have to endure ridicule. To her surprise, rather than wearing a mocking gaze, he wore a smile.

"That a duke who had the finest tutors cannot see," he finished. "Perhaps I shall learn from you after all. That is, if you will agree to teach me."

She smiled. This man might be on the verge of a storm at every turn, but she realized he also had a good heart. "Yes, I believe I will."

***

It soon became apparent that the work Emma would be required to do in order to sort out the mess that made up what the duke considered organization would take a fair amount of time. She had spent several hours sifting through various receipts, letters, and notes that had been piled haphazardly on top of the desk.

Days alone would not be nearly enough time; in fact, it would take her weeks to get everything in order.

When the numbers began to run together and the words looked muddled, Emma knew it was time to quit for the day. Sighing, she leaned back in the chair and found the duke staring at her. She returned the smile given to her, and her mind wandered. What if this man were to ask her to marry him? She could keep his books for him as he conducted the day-to-day business. When his temper grew hot, she would help calm him, perhaps with a kiss.

Her body burned with heat as she imagined his strong arms holding her, his anger turning to passion as their lips danced together. Then his kisses would move down her neck, and she could feel the heat from his breath as he kissed down…

The door opened, and Emma started. She had still been staring at the duke, and he at her, and she could not help but wonder if he was thinking of her in the same manner.

"Your Grace," his butler said. "I apologize for interrupting, but Lady Babbitt has arrived."

"Lady Babbitt?"

The butler cleared his throat. "Yes, Your Grace. Your dinner engagement?"

Emma felt her heart drop to her feet as the illusions of her and the duke were swept away as if on the current of a heavy flood. What a fool she had been for thinking that a man of title would even consider her in a romantic sense. With shame and foolishness weighing her down, she gathered her meager belongings.

"I really should be going," she said as if what the butler had announced matter nothing to her. Yet, inside, she hurt. Why? She knew little about him beyond his ledgers — and the rumors concerning the manner in which he controlled his anger, of course. In all reality, what she did know of him she did not like. With the horrible temper he possessed, what could she possibly find attractive?

"Will you return?" he asked.

Emma paused. For some reason, he had taken on the appearance of a scared rabbit in need of protection. Yet, that was silly; from what would a man such as he be needing protection?

Then she smiled at her own foolishness. Of course he needed her;

that was the reason he had requested her aid. It had nothing to do with any sort of possibility for romance or marriage, and she had to keep such thoughts from her mind. No one lived on dreams alone.

"I will," she replied to his question. "May I ask one thing?" When he nodded agreement, she asked, "What is our current situation?"

"I beg your pardon?"

"The handling of your account? What is the situation on it? I have not yet explained the issues, but I will when I return. My question is regarding your account with my father."

"It is yours forever!" His eyes grew wide and he cleared his throat. "That is, the work you and your father do is appreciated, and I will not be taking my business elsewhere."

Relief rushed through Emma. She had somehow won him over, which was strange since she had yet to do anything beyond looking through a pile of papers and ledgers. She had never been one to look a given horse in the mouth.

The duke reached into his pocket and pulled out several notes, from which he took one and handed it to her. "Please, take this. For your troubles today."

Emma looked at the note with wide eyes as if it might bite her. "Your Grace," she gasped, "I cannot accept such an amount." He seemed adamant, for he took her hand, placed the note in it, and folded her fingers around it. She thought she would swoon; although his hand was large and strong, it was gentle. Much different than she would have expected.

"You must accept it," he said, his voice husky. "Thank you for the work you completed this day. When can I expect you again?" Then he paused and added, "Or will your father be returning soon?"

She swallowed hard. Was this his way of saying he appreciated her hard work but would still prefer her father? "I will return in two days," she replied. "If that is fine with you, of course. Unfortunately, my father is still detained in London and will be for some time."

"Yes, that will be acceptable," he said.

He had not released her hand, and she worried she would soon be lying on the floor with a bottle of smelling salts under her nose if he did not. Yet, when he gave her hand a gentle squeeze and released it, she only wished his grasp to return.

"Tell my driver the time he must collect you. I look forward to seeing you again."

"Thank you, Your Grace," Emma muttered, although it took great effort to speak with clarity.

The duke led her to the front door where the butler had her cloak and hat. The older man gave her a pleasant smile and opened the door for her, and she returned it easily. He seemed a kind soul, unlike so many other butlers with whom she had come into acquaintance over the years. Most were stuffy, self-absorbed men who thought much of themselves, but not Mr. Goodard, or so she had heard the duke call him.

As she settled into the seat of the carriage, she glanced out the window. The duke remained on the stoop, still smiling, and although the distance was great, she knew his eyes were on her once again.

And she found she did not mind in the slightest.

Chapter Eight

By all appearances, the evening was going quite well. Lucas and his guest, Lady Ingrid Babbitt, had dined on a lovely pheasant complemented by a dry white wine he had brought in from France. Lady Babbitt, or Ingrid as she preferred he call her, was pretty and alluring in the red gown that emphasized the swell of her bosom. Her blond hair was piled on top of her head and had more than likely taken several hours to style. Even the jewelry she wore was fit for the Queen.

Most men would find her attractive, yet Lucas was not most men. Granted, Ingrid had a striking beauty about her, but he found he was not attracted to her in the physical sense. The woman was thirty, a widow with a young son, and five years older than Lucas, and Lucas considered the young viscountess one of his closest friends and confidantes.

At one time he had contemplated courting her, but if he was to do such a thing, their friendship would have been lost, and he found it was much more important to him.

As they sat in the drawing room, he poured them each a brandy as she continued with a recounting of a confrontation with one of her servants.

"It was then when I realized how accommodating I had been to him," she said with a sad sniff. "I will not tolerate those below me to act in such a way in my presence. I simply will not stand for it!" Lucas walked over to where she sat on the sofa and handed her the drink. "Thank you," she said with a smile.

Although Lucas enjoyed spending time with the woman, there were times, such as now, when her ramblings could drive him mad. They had arranged this dinner together several weeks before, and he had no reason to be rude to her.

"What is your servant to do now?" he asked. To him, the answer was simple; a servant was as replaceable as a broken vase as far as he was concerned. Where there was one person in a position in his household, ten more people waited anxiously for that one to leave, either of his or her own accord or by order of the duke himself.

She gave a derisive sniff. "I do not know nor care," she replied. "I have other things on which to concern myself." She sighed. "As a widow with a son off at boarding school, I find my mind only on business. Mother wishes me to remarry, but I have yet to find a man who can replace Joshua." She removed a kerchief from her sleeve and dabbed at the corner of her eye. "I apologize. It was not my intention to burden you with my troubles."

"You have nothing for which to apologize," he said with a smile, although a stab of guilt tore through him for his moment of annoyance with her. She was desperate for someone in which she could confide, and he was not acting much the friend. No, his mind was elsewhere, and he would have suffered great embarrassment if she knew his mind was elsewhere.

He glanced at the clock. Hours had passed since Miss Barrington had left his house, and yet it felt like years. It was strange that he missed the woman, more than he should by any right. She was no more than an extension of his bookkeeper, a man who served him. She was not a woman of title or wealth, and she had no right to invade his thoughts as she did.

"What bothers you, Lucas?" Ingrid asked, surprising him. He should not have been surprised; the woman always seemed to know when he was not in his right mind.

He sighed. "Oh, nothing. Some business matters is all." That was a mere half-truth, but at least it was truth. "Nothing to speak of, and certainly nothing with which to concern yourself." He had to find another subject on which to focus. "Concerning the property in Langley, have you decided to sell?"

Ingrid laughed. "I fear that if I sell it to you, you will no longer have a need to speak with me."

"Now, you know that is not true," he said in reply. "We have conducted many deals together and have still remained friends. There is no reason to think this sale would change our relationship any more than the others."

The landholdings left by the Viscount of Drudly were vast, and Ingrid and her son were set for life. He knew of the rumors about the woman — that she had sent off her young son of ten to boarding school to allow her the opportunity to find a new husband. Or that she was hoping to marry a man even higher in standing than the viscount in order to gain his estates, as well.

As far as Lucas was concerned, it was all rubbish; Ingrid had loved Joshua and still mourned him five years later, even if she no longer wore mourning clothes to show her loss. Lucas had seen the love they shared with his own eyes, and it pained him how the *ton* felt the need to muddy his good name by speaking poorly of his widow.

"I do have a request, if I may," Ingrid said with a smile.

"Of course," Lucas replied. "Anything."

"Lord Gates is hosting a party next month, and it is rumored that that horrid Lord Townsend might ask me to accompany him." She gave him a pout. "Save me from being forced to go with him by taking me yourself?"

He laughed. She had used that same pout to get her way with Joshua when he was alive. He hated to admit it, but it worked with him almost as well.

"I will even sell you the Langley property if you do," she added. "Then you will get something from it, as well." He pretended to consider the offer, to which she responded by throwing a napkin at him. "Oh, you!" she said in mock exasperation.

He laughed again. "Very well, we have a deal." He held out his hand, which she took and shook it as firmly as any man would have.

"Indeed, we have a deal, Your Grace," she said with a mischievous smile.

"Your Grace?" he asked.

"Well, you do tend to be in a mood so often that it is difficult to know how I should address you." Her eyes twinkled playfully as she spoke. "I find that, when conducting business with you, it would be best if I address you as such, for it seems to please you."

He chuckled. "You know me very well. I did not realize we were discussing business. Did we not plan to attend a party together?"

"In exchange for allowing you to purchase that property about which you have been asking for over two months," she replied with feigned haughtiness. "Therefore, it is a business arrangement. You will attend the party with me in exchange for the property."

"I will do no such thing," he said. "I will pay you for that land at the going rate and still accompany you to the party."

"You do drive a hard bargain, Your Grace," she said with a sigh. "To think that I also must allow you to give me money as well as be in my company...." She shook her head. "How difficult it is to get my friend to accompany me anywhere these days."

Lucas gaped at her. "You know that my attending the party with you has nothing to do with the land deal. I would never—"

She threw her head back and laughed. "Oh, Lucas, you are just too easy to fool!" She leaned in and kissed his cheek. "Thank you for accepting my invitation. And I am well aware that one is not dependent upon the other."

He let out a sigh of relief. "You definitely tricked me," he said with a laugh.

"Good. It keeps you at the ready." She stood. "I will have my solicitor draw up the papers. Perhaps we might have another dinner to finalize the transaction? That is, if you still allow a guest to call more than once a year?"

"I believe that can be arranged," Lucas said with a laugh. He walked her outside and opened the carriage door for her.

"Thank you for a lovely evening," she said. She accepted his aid into the carriage and sat back into the cushions on the bench. "Know that I enjoy every time we are able to get together."

"As do I," he said with a smile. "My mind as of late..." His voice trailed off as images of Emma appeared in his mind.

"Has been focused on business, I know," Ingrid finished for him, although it was not what he had meant to say. Yet, it was appropriate enough he did not correct her. "You are far too young to waste your life on worry. Promise me you will take care of yourself."

Lucas smiled. "I promise," he replied. "And you, as well."

"I always take care of myself," she said as she jutted her chin in clear defiance of any argument he might put forth. This, of course, made him laugh, and he closed the door with a shake to his head. She had been, and always would be, a great friend.

Ingrid was correct in one thing — he would wake up one day and realize he was an old man. Perhaps attending the party with her would be good for him. Not for meeting a woman. Not yet, anyway. For he was not ready for marriage — there was too much to do before he settled.

Furthermore, he could not keep his mind off Miss Barrington for long enough to enjoy the company of another woman.

***

Lucas was unsure how long he was outside, but he had walked over to a waiting bench placed under a tree just outside the front door of the house, his mind reviewing the events of the day. Or more specifically, reviewing Miss Emma Barrington.

What was it about her that made him feel so…? Hmm. What did he feel about the woman? The greater question was, could such feelings be permitted for a woman of her station by a man of his? Certainly, many dukes were known to cavort with women of the working and lower classes, but he was not many dukes. He was the Duke of Rainierd, and he did not lower his standards for a simple tryst with any woman. Despite his idea of decency, he found himself attracted to a bookkeeper's daughter. His father would have been outraged.

Eventually, the door opened and Goodard exited, a glass of brandy in each hand. Bonehedge Estates was located a fair distance from the village and, therefore, received few visitors. With no other family members left to whom he could speak to, Lucas had taken Goodard into his confidence.

At first, the old butler had been beside himself with concern for overstepping his place. After Lucas ordered the man to join him for a drink, the butler had obeyed. It was satisfying to have a male companion with whom he could confide, and Goodard proved to be a very capable companion.

"You have been listening in on my thoughts again?" Lucas asked as the old man handed him one of the glasses. "Well, come and sit beside me if you wish." Although Lucas had gotten the butler to share in a drink, he still would not sit without Lucas asking him first.

"As you wish, Your Grace." Goodard's knee cracked as he took a rigid seat beside Lucas, but he made no complaint. He had not changed much since Lucas first recalled knowing him, which was over twenty years before, when the man had been head footman. Regardless, it was times like this where the faithful butler provided a sort of friendship Lucas appreciated. "You grow quiet for a man with much attention drawn to him."

Lucas laughed. "Have I not always been this way, Goodard?"

The butler gave an appreciative nod. "Indeed, Your Grace. You have not had so many women vying for your attention, at least not since you were eighteen and made your first journey to London during the London season." He gave Lucas a wide grin.

"You do enjoy bluntness, do you not?"

"Of course, Your Grace," Goodard replied with an almost regal tone. "In most instances, being blunt is the only course of action."

Lucas took a sip of his brandy and sat back on the bench. "You are right, of course, about the women. Ingrid is a friend and nothing more." He eyed the man for a moment. "Unless you are speaking of Miss Barrington. I can assure you; she is here only to help me with the books. You know how dismal my bookkeeping skills are."

"I see, Your Grace," Goodard said. "And Lady Babbitt? She is a woman of wealth. You two are already good friends; an excellent start to something else perhaps?"

"Ingrid is wise, strong, and determined in her ways," he said with a laugh. "And before you mention her beauty, allow me to stop you there. Yes, most men find her beautiful, but she is not for me."

"You find her beautiful but have no interest?"

"I have no interest in her beyond friendship." He shook his head. "I feel nothing for her. I understand that love can grow, but we have been friends for much too long to ruin it by throwing love, or even courtship, into the mix. No, it would be best if we maintained our current relationship as it is."

"I understand," Goodard replied. "And Miss Barrington? What of her?"

Lucas took another sip of his brandy to give himself not only a moment to think of a reply, but to allow the fire of the drink to put his thoughts into perspective. "I do not know her. She is kind, highly intelligent, and one might see her as beautiful."

"One might?" the butler asked. "But you, Your Grace?"

"See her as beautiful?" When the older man nodded, Lucas replied, "Why, yes, of course. She is a delicate creature to be sure. She has a fire inside her that burns so brightly…" He sighed. "When she releases it, it is as though she could stop the wind from blowing, and yet, she controls it so well."

It became quiet, their attention lying out into the darkness of the trees. Lucas wondered if Goodard would speak again, if he would give some sort of wondrous advice as he had in the past, and when he spoke again, Lucas felt a sense of relief.

"Before I came to work for your father, I was an apprentice to a blacksmith."

Lucas turned toward the stoic man, shocked at this revelation. "Were you really? I did not know!"

"Oh, yes," Goodard replied with a light chuckle. "The blacksmith with whom I was apprenticed said I had great potential. I dreamed of opening my own forge, and from there taking on other apprentices. In my mind's eye, I imagined people coming from all over England to witness my great skills." Lucas laughed, as did Goodard. Then the old man shook his head. "I had been married only a month, and I was gone from sunrise to sunset every day. To me, it was the only way to reach the grand ideal I had created in my head. She rarely complained, but when she did, I assured her that one day, I would have enough money, and then we would spend all our time together." He gave a heavy sigh, and sadness filled his features. "I never expected her to fall ill."

"I am sorry," Lucas said. "I did not know. I am certain you still miss her."

"I do. Yet I do not tell you this story to garner pity. I wish you to know that life is precious. You believe your future is laid out before you, but you do not know what may come. You are but five and twenty today, but tomorrow, you will be thirty."

Lucas considered the butler's words. "I believe I understand, but I am unsure as to your point."

"Your anger over the loss of your parents, especially your father, has driven you to consume yourself with work. Perhaps it is time to begin thinking of finding someone to love."

Taking a deep breath, Lucas let it out slowly in an attempt to calm himself. Although what the old man said was true, it did not mean Lucas liked it. "I do worry that my anger is so great at times that I will scare away any woman. Apparently, everyone — rich or poor — knows of my temper and have placed upon me the moniker of the Duke of Storms."

Goodard stood and took the empty glass from Lucas. "Then, might I recommend you find someone to calm it, Your Grace, before it is too late. If you desire a woman, tell her. Spend every moment you can with her. If not, you will live to regret it." With a sad look, he gave a diffident bow and returned to the house, the wall between stations put back into place between them.

Lucas looked up at the stars. The wisdom given this night was great, and it gave him much on which to think. For the storm inside consumed him, and he wondered if Miss Barrington would be able to calm it.

Or if such a task was even something she wished to accomplish.

Chapter Nine

Upon entering the office in Bonehedge Estates, Emma noticed three things. The first was the extra chair that had been situated beside the desk. The second was the dark blue coat that fit the duke quite well, as did his breeches and stockings, which allowed a pleasant view of his well-formed calf. The third and final thing she noticed was the smile he wore. Perhaps it was a trick of the sunlight streaming in from the window, but his smile seemed to radiate around the room.

"I take it your journey was without incident," the duke said as he moved away from the window.

Emma dropped him a quick curtsy before replying, "Yes, Your Grace. Thank you again for your kindness in sending a carriage for me."

He came to stop in front of her, and for some odd reason, her breathing became labored. Was it growing hot in the room? She glanced at the fireplace, wondering why he would have a fire lit in the middle of the summer, only to find it empty. She wished she had thought to bring a fan with her.

"I am happy to be of assistance," he said with a smile. "Please, sit. I have set up another chair so I may watch and learn." Then he surprised Emma by walking around the desk and pulling out the chair for her.

As if in a haze, she walked over and sat in the chair, the duke pushing it forward. It was all so strange, but Emma smiled at him, nonetheless. "Thank you," she murmured.

Inside, all she could wonder was, *Who is this man? He certainly is not the same man I called upon two days ago.*

The duke sat in the extra chair, a high-backed piece that clearly had not been designed for comfort, and when he turned that smile on her, the haze around her thickened. Her cheeks burned, and she had to shake her head to clear it. She was here for business, not for some imagined tryst with a duke, handsome or not. If she had any sort of contemplations that something more might come out of this arrangement, she only had to remind herself of the lady guest who had arrived to have dinner with him to bring her back to reality. That and the fact he was a duke and she a simple bookkeeper's daughter. The latter was more prevalent than the former by far.

"The last time I was here," she said, attempting to keep her voice from shaking, "I spoke of your penmanship. May I ask why it appears rushed?"

"I believe the task of bookkeeping a bore," the duke replied. "And your observations are correct. I find myself rushing to take down notes or enter the amounts."

Emma nodded and then turned to him. She had to tread lightly, for her next words could be taken in a much different manner than she intended. "You employ the services of my father, and yet you find the need to keep your own accounts. May I ask why?"

"It is a reasonable question," he replied as he sat back in the chair. "The truth of the matter is, I find the need for two sets of books in case...well, any thievery was to take place." He raised a hand as if in defense. "Not you or your father," he said with a chuckle. "It is a practice my father taught me." He went quiet, and then he shook his head as if clearing an unwanted thought. "I need not rush, and I must improve on my penmanship. Is that correct?"

"That would be a good start," Emma replied, unsure if she should be offended or if she should laugh. This man was a contradiction in himself. Yet, as she gazed into his eyes, she found it difficult to pull away. What would happen if she were to stand, lose her footing, and end up in his arms? She blinked. From where had that thought come?

She cleared her throat. "I will also ask that you trust me," she continued, surprised that her voice was even. What she had expected was a tiny squeak rather than the calm tone that she was able to produce.

What was wrong with her? If she did not put her thoughts in order soon, the possibility of her losing this precious account was certain!

Placing a finger on the sum at the bottom of the page that was open before her, she said, "What you have calculated for this account is forty pounds more than what I calculated."

The duke leaned forward and his arm brushed hers. He did not seem to notice, but Emma certainly did, for heat radiated through her body and her throat became parched. She tried to bring moisture to her mouth, but her mouth had become as arid as a desert.

"How do you know my numbers are not correct?" he asked. "What if the error is on your part?"

Summoning all her strength, Emma managed to produce words as she pointed to a number on the page. "This here. Look how the nine is written when in fact it is—"

"An eight," he said before dropping back in his chair as if in shock. "I presume that is not the only error you found?"

Emma smiled. "I am sorry to be the bearer of bad news," she moved her finger to another digit on the page, "but you can see a similar mistake here, and here, as well." She glanced up to find the duke not studying the notations but instead, studying her. "Your Grace?"

"Yes?" he asked before giving a start and returning his attention to the ledger. "I see now."

Emma wondered if he did, indeed, see the errors, but she realized it did not matter, for she would be paid either way.

"I find it amazing."

"I beg your pardon?" she asked.

"The way you understand numbers. It is a gift, I would say."

"I do have an aptitude for them," she said, enjoying the compliment. "I suppose I always have."

"Tell me about—"

The door opened, and a man in livery entered the room and stopped with a gasp. "Oh, forgive me, Your Grace!" he said, his eyes wide. "I thought you were not here."

The duke stood, rage etched on his features. "Never again open that door when it is closed!" he shouted at the poor man, who cowered in fear. "Do you understand? Never again!"

"My apologies, Your Grace," the man murmured, his back hunched as if expecting to be struck at any moment. "Truly, I am sorry." He backed out the door, still mumbling apologies in that cowed manner, much like a dog with its tail between its legs after it has lived a life of abuse.

When the door closed, the duke returned to his chair as if nothing was amiss. "My apologies. Please, continue. What other errors have you found?"

For the next few hours, Emma explained the basic management of numbers, how to organize his receipts and letters, all the time wondering if it was time for the lessons to end lest his anger became directed toward her. Gone were the fleeting images of possible romance, all replaced by thoughts of this man striking her with his fists; although, not once did he grow angry or frustrated with her.

***

Closing the ledger, Emma stood and knuckled her back. They had been at it for several hours, and the hour was growing late. Although she had been concerned he would grow angry with her, he had not. Instead, he had upheld the pleasant behavior he had before the entry of the servant. She did not allow the shield to fall, for, although his presence captivated her, his temper appalled her. Furthermore, he had an interest in the woman who had dined with him earlier in the week.

Emma laughed silently. Even if the other woman had not been present, Emma would never have a chance with a man of the duke's position. To allow such thoughts to overcome her was a useless waste of time, of which she had little.

"I believe there is nothing more with which I can aid you," she said as she turned to him. This, of course, was not completely true; he did need to learn to control his temper, but she was not the person to help him in that arena. She was a simple bookkeeper, not a governess nor an instructor of etiquette. "To continue instructing you would be unfair and only a way to extort money from you, which I would not do."

"I see," he replied as he tapped his chin. "Allow me to pay you for your time today." He reached into his coat pocket and produced a ten-pound note. "Please do not argue this time."

"Very well," Emma said as she took the note from him. When her hand brushed his, she swallowed hard and put the note into her pocket. "Your generosity is great, and I thank you for it." This would be more than enough to pay the past rent and a little left over, which she would put away for the next month's rent.

When she looked back up at him, he was staring at her again. This time she saw sorrow behind his eyes. "I believe that, if all of your ledgers are delivered to me from now on, there will be no more discrepancies. I do not mean any disrespect toward your father, but if a bookkeeper cannot be trusted to keep accurate records and not cheat his clients, then that bookkeeper does not deserve to retain his office."

"I agree," the duke said. "And I will send you everything I have."

He stepped aside, and Emma walked past him. Although she wished to return home, she found it difficult to leave. "If you need my assistance any further or have any questions, I am here for you." Her voice was just above a whisper, and she berated herself, for she sounded like a foolish child. "Goodbye." She hurried to the door but stopped when he called out.

"Miss Barrington." His voice was a near-panic. "I have a question for you."

She closed her eyes for a moment and then turned back around to face him.

"The day you came here in lieu of your father?"

"Yes?" she said, her heart racing. Would he inquire after her father again? She hoped not, for it was a discussion she did not wish to have.

"I...lost my temper that day, which I am apt to do. Yet, you came back through that door. You stood before me and spoke straightforwardly."

He was angry with her for speaking against him! She really did need to learn how to stay her tongue or she would be ousted!

"I apologize for my outburst, Your Grace," she said. "I did not mean to disrespect—"

"No. I am not seeking an apology from you." He took a step closer.

"I saw the hurt in your eyes, and yet you did not weep. How was it that you were able to control your emotions? Or why did you do so?"

Emma found his questions strange, and she struggled to understand if he was angry with her or curious. His inquiry seemed sincere, and judging from the tone of his voice, he was not angry. Therefore, she chose to be honest in her reply. "As a woman, I am told I cannot conduct business as a man would," she began and then paused as she tried to collect her thoughts. "I admit that it was not only that."

"Please, continue."

She sighed. "The fact of the matter is, your temper terrified me, I cannot deny that. My love of the business, for my father, takes precedence. In order to maintain what we have, I must speak my mind, even if it brings about the anger of the person with whom I am speaking." She glanced down at the floor. Discussing her personal feelings with someone else had never been easy. Friends assumed time she did not have. "As for my tears, they are my own, and I fear that, if I had released them while in your presence, I would have lost your respect."

The room went silent, and Emma looked up to see the duke studying her.

"You have gained my respect in more ways than you can know," he said. "The ability to control your own storm is an admirable trait I must learn." He reached out and took hold of her hand. "Miss Barrington, as you have witnessed, a storm brews inside me, an anger I struggle to control. Would you teach me to quell this disturbance within me?"

"I-I do not know how I would be able to do such a thing."

"Be in my company. Allow me to observe you, to learn from you." He released her hand and the sadness returned to his face. "I realize this is a strange request, but I do ask it, nonetheless. Of course, I will pay you for your services."

Emma considered his offer. What could she do? It truly was a strange request. She did not control her emotions as well as he thought, but after considering the manner in which he had treated the servant earlier, she was better prepared than he.

She had agreed to accompany the baron to the party in order to keep the office; how was this any different? And the duke would be paying her for her services, money she needed desperately.

"Very well," she replied. "I will continue to help you in any way I can, but I cannot make any promises."

"Wonderful," the duke said. "I look forward to learning more from you."

Emma could not help thinking that she, too, looked forward to their time together.

Chapter Ten

Stephen trembled as Emma helped him don his new coat. She had decided to use the money the duke had given her to purchase the item for Stephen, which in turn would allow him to converse with other shopkeepers. It was a gamble, but it was one she had to take, and she hoped the former drunk would be able to make contact with new clients who would be willing to use the services offered by her office. The point of the matter was they certainly would not discuss turning over business accounts with a man in ragged clothing. And certainly not a woman regardless of what clothing she wore.

"What if I fail you?" he asked in a shaky voice. "You've done so much for me, and all I'll do is disappoint you." He looked down at the ground, and Emma could not help but feel her heart swell for him.

She reached out and took his hand. "I am proud of the accomplishments you have made in the past year. I must admit that I am hurt you believe me to be a fool."

His head shot up, and he gaped at her. "You ain't...aren't a fool! I would never think of even suggesting such a thing about you!"

She sniffed derisively. "Only a fool would buy a man a new coat and send him to conduct business if she did not believe in his capabilities." When the old man brightened, she added, "I trust you, Stephen. I know in my heart that you are a good man, one who can converse with many with skill." She squeezed his hands and sighed. "To be honest, you are my last hope to save the business. Will you at least make an attempt? For me?"

"Yes, Miss Emma. I'll try."

Smiling, she leaned forward and placed a small kiss on his rough cheek. "Thank you, Stephen. You know where to go first, correct?"

"I do," he said, smoothing his jacket, although it had no wrinkles. "The new millinery shop and then to the butcher's." He walked past her and stopped at the door. "I suppose I should wish you luck, too."

"Luck?"

"With the Duke of Storms. If he harms you in any way, you let me know and I'll take care of it." He lifted his hand in a fist, and Emma's heart went out to him. His arthritis was so bad, he could not close it completely, but it was the kind of love he had for her that she cherished. His words, his actions, they were what she needed, but more importantly, he was there when she needed a friend.

"I know," she said with a smile. "Now, off with you." He gave her a cheeky grin and then left, and Emma returned to the small desk. Memories flooded her mind, causing a few tears to well in her eyes. She recalled being no older than eight, her father hunched over this same desk with candlelight highlighting his features. He would look up at her and smile, outstretch his arms, and pull her in tight. He always told her how much she was loved. As time went by, she studied under him, learning to read, write, and understand numbers, and he always said how proud he was at her quick wit.

As she ran her hand over the old wooden desk, she sighed heavily. "I will not fail you," she whispered. "Stephen is procuring more work for us. The business will be fine; you will see."

A movement from outside the window caught her eye, and she recognized the carriage the duke had sent for her before come to a stop in front of the office. Although she knew he would never see her as she saw him — a person capable of succeeding — it was nice to dream.

***

"I hope you do not mind accompanying me," the duke said as Emma walked beside him. He had asked her to join him for a stroll, and although she thought it a strange request, she accepted.

She had to admit the gardens had been a curiosity to her since her first time there; therefore, it gave her the opportunity to see what it had to offer. "It is far too lovely today to remain inside; something Goodard reminds me I do all too often."

Emma smiled. "I do not mind."

And she spoke the truth. She had never seen so many colors of flowers in one place before, and there were some varieties that were new to her. One might have thought it strange that she did not know the names of flowers, but she spent the majority of her days stuck inside a dreary office working with numbers. It was only on rare occasions she ventured out to enjoy what nature had to offer.

"And what are those?" she asked, pointing to a bed filled with dark red and pink flowers.

"Those are Sweet Williams."

She stopped and stared at him. "Surely you jest!" she said with a gasp. "Why on Earth would anyone give a flower such a name?"

He laughed. "I have no idea, but that is what they are called. I have to admit, I find the name strange myself, but I suppose I have no right to change the name of a flower simply because I do not prefer the name it was given."

"No, I suppose you are right," she replied with a light laugh.

Several gardeners worked at various tasks, some pulling weeds while others trimmed the maze of hedges. At the end of one path rose a large bush, taller than even the duke, with light purple flowers.

"And those?" she asked, hoping he would not tire of her questions. She was uncertain why she felt at ease asking, but she could not stop herself. Her father had admonished her — playfully, of course — on more than one occasion for her propensity to inquire about anything and everything that piqued her fancy.

"Those are called lilacs," the duke replied, clearly amused by her inquiries.

She touched the tiny petals. "So, these are lilacs. I have heard of them, for I once was given a soap that had the scent of lilac, but I did not know that these were the flowers from which it came."

They continued the stroll, passing a gardener who stopped to bow as they walked past. Emma offered him a smile, and he looked back at her with shock, as if he had never received such a response.

This made her sad; everyone deserved a smile from time to time, even if he was a servant.

Although Emma did not want their time to come to an end, the hour was growing late. The carriage had not stopped in front of the Barrington office until just past two, and after arriving at Bonehedge Estates, she had been forced to wait more than an hour as the duke finished a meeting. She still was unsure what he expected of her on this new venture, but he would be paying her for her time, and she needed the money. Therefore, she said nothing.

"My father was like me," he said as they came to a stop along the path. "Or rather, I am like him. He was too busy to enjoy the gardens, or anything else, for that matter. Yet, during those rare occasions I do come out here, I find myself not wanting to leave." He laughed. "You would think I would spend more time out here than I do."

"I understand," Emma replied. "Not that I have ever had a garden, but I have always wanted one." She chewed her bottom lip. "I apologize. I do not mean to complain, for I have had a good life."

"No. Please, tell me more about your life. I would enjoy hearing your story."

"Well, although we never had a garden of our own, my father allowed me to join him at times when he delivered ledgers to clients. If they had a child, sometimes I would be allowed to join him or her in their garden. It was an experience I always cherished. It has been many years since I've had such an opportunity." She looked around her and then back at the duke. "You have all of this; I would suggest you make time to enjoy it."

"That sounds more a command than a suggestion," he said with a raised eyebrow.

Emma felt fear grip her for a moment. Would he become angry with her? "I did not mean offense."

He laughed. "No offense was taken," he said. "You are the instructor and I am the pupil; I should be obeying your commands, should I not?" He wore a mischievous grin, and Emma could not help but return it.

"Then I shall not offer any apologies from this day forward."

They continued their stroll until they came to a fence at the far end of the garden. Emma stopped, her eyes widening. "Oh, Your Grace, the views! They are marvelous!" As far as she could see, rolling green hills covered in yellow and white flowers stretched before her. How could such vistas have existed so close to her home and she had never seen them?

"I agree," he said as he stood beside her. "When I was a child, I would explore those fields in search of all sorts of treasure." He sighed and shook his head. "What a silly thing to believe I could find hidden treasures."

"It is not silly," Emma admonished. "It is in our imagination where our dreams lie. There is nothing silly about having dreams."

"I find myself learning from you with each word you speak," he said as he gazed down at her. She knew she had to be as red as the Sweet Williams they had left in the flowerbed behind them. "You have such a wonderful outlook on life, so bright and encouraging. How do you do that despite your business struggling?"

Although she knew he meant no offense, she found it difficult to answer. How did one explain hope to one who had everything he could ever want? How did one explain faith to one who did not have to rely on it in order to live?

"Have I asked too much?"

Emma smiled. "No. It is a complicated question is all." She turned to look at the hills. "The truth is, if I accept that which lies before me, the weight will cause me to sink beneath a storm of sorrow. I cannot allow that to happen, not for me and especially not for my father."

"Your love for him is admirable. Your willingness to help with his business speaks of the strength of your relationship with him. He has taught you well."

"He has," Emma replied. A hot tear rolled down her cheek, although she had tried to keep it from escaping. "I am sorry. I suppose I cannot keep all of my emotions in check all of the time."

She went to wipe away the tear, but the duke reached up and brushed his thumb against her cheek. "I understand," he whispered. "In my own way, I find myself trying to impress my father." He gave a small snort. "Although he has been dead for some time now, I still feel the need to please him. I want him to see that his son is not a failure."

His words shocked Emma. This man, by all appearances, was strong and capable. She would never have guessed he felt about himself so. "Although I do not know you well, I do not believe you are a failure."

The duke offered her a smile, but she could see the sadness in it.

"That is a command, not a suggestion," she added with a small smile.

They laughed before they returned their gaze to the hills, where they stood for several minutes enjoying the quiet solitude that surrounded them.

***

Emma remained in the garden with the duke for what she estimated was more than an hour, and as they made their way back to the house, they discussed the best time and day for Emma to return.

"My schedule is busy over the next four days," the duke said as he walked beside her. "Are you available on Saturday? Say, around two?"

"Yes, that would be fine." She still was unsure what they had accomplished this day, but she had enjoyed herself regardless. The strange thing was, although she had sworn off any thoughts of him as any sort of romantic interest, she could not help but secretly wish he would kiss her. It made no sense whatsoever, but she could not stop the images from playing in her head. He had been nothing but kind to her, and the strange images of them together kept flickering in her mind. And although it was against her better judgment, she allowed them their brief moments, if only to experience the chance at love. Not the reality, she was certain, but that small chance something might grow between them.

As they entered through the rear door of the house, they came upon the butler and a woman who Emma thought was the most beautiful she had ever seen. She had flowing blond locks and wore a purple gown that emphasized the swell of her breasts and her small waist. The jewelry the woman wore could have purchased the building in which her father's office was located, the room in which she lived, and a carriage thrown in for good measure.

"Lucas!" the woman said as she waited for him and Emma to approach. She kissed him on the cheek and asked, "Is this the new servant you employed?"

Emma's cheeks burned in shame. Of course she would believe her a servant. Never had Emma owned a dress half as exquisite as what this woman wore.

"No, Ingrid," the duke replied. "Allow me to present Miss Emma Barrington. Her father keeps my books for me, and Emma is his assistant. Miss Barrington, this is Lady Ingrid Babbitt, Viscountess of Drudly and a dear friend of mine."

The woman offered Emma a smile. "My apologies." Before Emma could respond, Lady Babbitt turned back to the duke as if dismissing Emma outright. "You did not forget our dinner, did you?" How could the woman ever be taken seriously with such a pout on her lips?

The duke laughed. "No, I did not. I have been busy…"

Emma felt her stomach sicken as she stopped listening to their conversation. Standing beside Lady Babbitt, she felt the inferiority of her position as much as the plainness of who she was. It was no wonder the duke had an interest in this woman, for she was everything any man could want. Emma recalled her name as being the woman who had arrived for dinner previously, and she felt out of place in their presence, as if she were intruding on their intimate moment.

What sickened her the most was that she had once again allowed thoughts of her and this man as a couple to intrude on her sensibilities. His words to her were that of kindness. What was it about the Duke of Rainierd that had her mind soaring on flights of fancy? She had always been a reasonable woman, and yet this man made her feel a young girl struck with infatuation! She had to stop the foolishness, for it would only lead to heartbreak. And Emma had no time for such trivialities.

"Forgive me, Your Grace, for taking you away from your schedule," she said, not even taking note on whether or not she was interrupting. "I must be on my way back to the office. Lady Babbitt, it was a pleasure meeting you." She dipped a quick curtsy. "Good evening."

She forced herself to walk out to the carriage, stopping only long enough to gather her cloak and hat from the butler. Goodard gave her a kind smile, which she returned readily. He seemed a nice man, and was welcoming, for which she was glad, for although the duke was behaving himself thus far, she had seen how his demeanor could change at the drop of a hat. At least Goodard seemed a man she could count on for consistency, or so she hoped.

Once the carriage moved down the drive, she allowed herself a moment of relief. Never again would she put herself in the position to believe she had more with a man than she first thought. Be he duke or baron, it did not matter, for she had her heart to protect.

Chapter Eleven

L ucas stared out the window of the drawing room. It had been hours since Miss Barrington had left, and although the night outside was dark and lonely, he could still feel her presence around him. It was a light that provided warmth and comfort, far better than the brandy he drank this evening.

Ingrid came to stand beside him. "Does my conversation bore you?"

He sighed. "No, you do not bore me. My apologies; my mind has been elsewhere this evening. You know how I get when I have business concerns."

Ingrid chuckled. "I think you have more than business concerns on your mind," she said. "Am I correct in saying so?"

He raised his glass and took a drink. She had always been good at reading his thoughts and spoke with him without restriction. It was strange now being alone with her, even as a friend. If he were asked to explain why, he was unsure he could, but a feeling of unfaithfulness surrounded him. It made no sense, for he and Miss Barrington had no relationship beyond a business arrangement, but it was there, nonetheless.

Sharing such sentiments with a woman of the *ton*, a woman who would not understand this strange infatuation he had with a common woman, was out of the question, regardless of how much he considered her a friend. "Perhaps," he replied to her question. "Or it could be that I am only thinking of work."

71

"I have told you often that you are too consumed with work, have I not?" When he nodded his agreement, she continued. "Now, I will not have you thinking of business. You should think of pleasure. Enjoy yourself for once in your life."

She pulled him by the arm, indicating he should follow her. The only place she could be leading him was the couch, a much too intimate place for two people who were simply friends. Granted, they had shared the same couch on several occasions over the years, but tonight felt somehow different.

He swallowed hard. No, they were not going to the couch, for she led him past it. Beyond it was the cart that held several crystal decanters of spirits. Was Ingrid attempting to seduce him? Never before had she attempted such a thing, but he stared at her hand in horror. He had to put a stop to this madness before it went too far!

"Ingrid, enough," he murmured as images of the bookkeeper's daughter flashed in his mind. The stricken look on Miss Barrington's face if he were to share even a kiss with this woman. The hurt it would cause her. It was all silly, for she had not indicated she had any feelings for him, but he could not stop the explosion of anger that erupted in him. "Ingrid! I said enough!"

Ingrid backed into the nearby bookcase as if afraid. "Lucas? What have I done?"

"You are my friend, and we have conducted business together, but trying to fill me with brandy and have your way with me is unacceptable and beneath you!" His breathing was heavy, and his face burned with anger.

Yet Ingrid said nothing; she simply shook her head.

"Do not ever try that again."

She sighed heavily. "I only wanted you to read a book I recently read and thoroughly enjoyed. I thought it might bring you pleasure." Indeed, in her hand she held a book, and guilt rushed through him. He had misread her intentions, had taken her words and actions in a direction he had never considered before, and he was ashamed of himself beyond measure

"I do not know what to say," he whispered. "I can only apologize for my outburst. I had thought you meant to…" His words trailed off as he realized how silly they sounded.

"To seduce you?" She finished for him. Walking past him, she placed her wine glass on the table. "To think I would make such an attempt hurts me more than you will ever know. We have been friends for many years. I know what others believe, I know the rumors, but I never thought you believed them, as well." She gave him a sad look and then walked to the door.

"Ingrid, please," he called after her. "Forgive me. I do not know why I reacted in such a manner."

The woman smoothed her skirts and took a deep breath. "Many times you have allowed me to be the recipient of your anger. I have endured it, trying to conduct business with you, but more importantly, to maintain our friendship. And after all this time, after all we have been through, you not only accuse me of seduction, but you also treat me like a common woman? Good evening to you, Your Grace."

"Ingrid!" he called out again, but she ignored him.

Lucas felt his chest tighten, almost as tight as when his parents had died. He doubled up his fist and drove it into the bookcase, but it brought him no relief, so he kicked a small table, the vase it held smashing to the floor. Then he went to the liquor card and overturned it, the crystal creating a lilting melody as it, too, shattered on the floor and mingled with the various liquids the decanters held. Letting out a roar, he went to his desk wondering if he had the strength to throw it out the window.

***

That night, as his servants cleaned up the disaster Lucas had made of his office — he had not thrown his desk out the window, it had been much too heavy to lift on his own — he stood out on the veranda staring out into the night. He could not see anything beyond the glowing patches that poured out the windows, but he did not care.

All his life, anger had consumed him, and he saw the result of what he could not control in the disapproving look his father gave him that matched how Ingrid looked at him tonight. He felt a fool for his constant misreading of situations, to always want to please and yet failing at every turn. The storm inside always raged no matter how hard he tried to bring it under control.

Then there was Miss Barrington. The mere thought of the woman seemed to soothe him, far more than the brandy that trickled down his throat. Her words, her smile, her simple presence created a calmness he needed. Although he had hired her to teach him better methods for keeping his books, he knew the truth. Somehow, she could see past his temper and see him for who he was.

No, that made no sense, for if he could not see past the storm inside him, how could a simple woman such as she? Therefore, the question still remained: Who was he?

For that matter, who was she? He was seeing her as a different person from the first time they had met, and that only confused him all the more. He took another drink of his brandy, his thoughts sorting through the muddled mess in his head that resembled the chaos he had handed her that first day she had gone over his ledgers.

He knew the truth, but he did not want to admit it; he had a growing attraction to her. The woman had strength of character and could settle a storm with her mere presence. A woman who had assisted her father despite the fact she was a woman. She had no title, no wealth, and yet she had a greater gift that blazed in her eyes. A calm, encouraging love, and he wanted it more than ever.

Chapter Twelve

M r. Theodore Bromley was an older man with wisps of fine, gray hair combed over the top of an otherwise bare head, and Emma found him pleasant during their conversation together.

"Although I do not partake in as much business as when I was younger," the man was saying as he sat across from Emma in her father's office, "I still have many holdings. My son has been slowly taking over, as he should, but I still maintain the bulk of the ledgers."

"Well, you will be happy to know that my father has been a bookkeeper in this area for many years," Emma replied with a smile. "You will not hear a negative word spoken against him."

He nodded. "And his assistant, Mr. Foreman is it?"

"That is correct," she said, stifling the laugh that tried to erupt. Stephen would be over the moon to hear a man in Mr. Bromley's place address him in such a manner.

"A fine gentleman," Mr. Bromley said. "I was never made to feel more welcomed in my life by a stranger. As a matter of fact," he looked around the room, "I almost expected it to be he who would be at this meeting if your father was absent."

Emma had to force herself from shouting at the man. When would men learn that women were as intelligent as they? "Unfortunately, Stephen...that is Mr. Foreman is otherwise indisposed or he would have been happy to meet with you."

Mr. Bromley stood, and Emma followed suit. "Send the man over Monday to collect my ledgers," he said as he straightened his coat.

His stomach was so large that he was unable to button it. "Will your father require payment beforehand?" He went to reach into his coat pocket, but Emma forestalled him.

"Payment is made upon delivery of your completed ledgers," Emma assured him. "That is how much stock we, that is my father puts into the work completed in this office."

"Excellent," he said with a wide grin. "That is exactly what I was hoping to hear. Good day, Miss Barrington."

Emma escorted him to the door, her heart racing with excitement. Mr. Bromley had moved into the area with his hat-making business, and Stephen had scooped the man up before another bookkeeper had even considered approaching him. Perhaps they would set a new precedent; if one wanted a client, one did not wait for him to come. One went out and caught him.

The best part was that this was the second client Stephen had brought to the office in the past two days, and he could not have been prouder. He peeked around the corner of a building across the street, and Emma motioned for him to return once Mr. Bromley was out of sight.

"Well?" Stephen asked, his hat clutched so tightly in his hands his fingers would forever be imprinted on it. "What did he say? Were you able to acquire him?"

"I was," Emma replied before squealing with delight. "You have been a wonder, Stephen! I must thank you for what you have done."

He turned three shades of red. "There's no need, Miss Emma," he replied, although his voice was choked. "It's an honor to help you."

After stepping inside, Emma crossed the room and reached into the drawer of her father's desk. Producing produced several coins, she placed them in Stephen's hand.

"Oh, no, Miss Emma," he said as he tried to return the farthings to her. "I don't need nothing...I mean, I don't need *any*thing. You've helped me out so much already."

She closed his fingers around the coins. "I would like for you to have a nice meal today. Call it a reward most fitting for what Mr. Bromley called 'a fine gentleman'."

Stephen's eyes almost covered his entire face they widened so. "A gentleman? I?" He looked down at the coins and then his new coat.

"I suppose I am at that!" He beamed so much he could have lit a darkened room.

He straightened his posture — and his hat, before placing it on his head — and grabbed his lapels with each hand. "A gentleman," he whispered. "Who'da thought?"

Emma giggled and then coughed to cover it. "Now, do not run off and get married on me," she teased. "I still need your help around here."

"No, I won't, I promise." Poor Stephen did not seem to catch her teasing tone. "I must admit, though, the women have smiled at me more since I've gotten my new coat." This seemed to baffle him as much as fill him with pride.

"You will be fighting them all off if you are not careful," Emma said.

This made him laugh, clearly catching the humor of her words this time. "Ah, now, Miss Emma," he said, blushing more now than he had earlier, "you know that ain't...isn't true." He stood taller and held his chin higher than she had ever seen from him in the past.

Emma looked around the room and smiled. Clients, and their money, were beginning to pour in and for the first time in a long time, she began to believe that her life would flourish once more.

***

The euphoria did not continue throughout the remainder of the day. Emma had arrived at Bonehedge manner as the duke had requested, and Goodard had led her to the gardens, where the duke was waiting. As she no longer needed to learn the names of the flowers or trees, they seemed to have little to discuss, and every attempt Emma made at beginning a conversation was met with grunts and off-hand comments. Soon, she fell into a silence that matched his, unsure what was expected of her.

It was on their second round that the duke finally spoke. "You appeared pleased when you first arrived," he said as the light breeze ruffled his hair. "What was the cause of such pleasure, if I might ask?"

Emma considered telling him that it was not his business to know her personal life, but she did not want to upset him. He was ripe for an outburst, and she could not add fire to the kindling. Perhaps it was the dark clouds that were gathering in the distance that seemed to strengthen him, but whatever it was, she had to tread lightly. "This week I have taken on two clients," she replied to his question. "For once, I feel there is hope ahead of me, when all there was before was darkness."

She glanced over at the man, who seemed to consider her words before giving a short nod. He made no reply, so she decided to use what had been their first true conversation as a means to learn what was troubling him, for something, indeed, was causing distress.

"You are unhappy," she said, attempting to keep her voice light. "Might I ask why?"

He turned to her, his eyes narrowed in anger. "Do not presume to know anything about me, Miss Barrington," he snapped.

She was taken aback at his harsh words, and she could not stop the fear that gripped her. She had seen only a glimpse of the storm that brewed in this man; would she learn the strength of his tempest now?

"I apologize, Your Grace," she said in a soft voice. "I did not mean any offense by my question."

He sighed heavily. "No, you did nothing wrong," he said. "The truth of the matter is I lashed out at a friend of mine earlier this week. I did not like what I heard, so I..." He paused and took a deep breath. "I grew angry."

He tightened his hand into a fist at his side, and Emma could see he was fighting down the urge to lash out again, even though nothing but a memory provoked him.

"She left in anger, and I wonder if I shall ever see her again." He glanced at Emma. "What do I do? Do I let her alone and see if she comes around? Or should I go to her and beg her forgiveness?"

Emma knew instantly of whom he spoke, for the 'she' could only have been Lady Babbitt. They must have had a lover's quarrel, something Emma had never experienced. How would a woman who had never been in love counsel anyone about such issues?

They stopped before the wondrous rolling hills, and Emma turned to look into the duke's eyes. How easy it would have been for her to advise him to not pursue this other woman. Doing so would benefit Emma and her selfishness. Although it pained her, the heart of this man belonged to another, and nothing she could say or do could make him look at her in such a manner.

"My advice would be to seek her out when you are ready and apologize for your actions. I believe she would forgive you if you did so." If it were she who sought his apology, she would forgive him.

"And if she does not accept my apology?" he asked. "What do I do then?"

His worry warmed her heart, for it proved the level of emotion that resided deep inside him. Yet, he allowed his anger to prevail over his life. He was in need of Emma's aid, and she was determined to do what she could to see he was successful in reining in his temper.

"You can do no more than that," she said. "It is in forgiveness that the storm inside you will calm." As she spoke, thunder rumbled in the distance as if to mock her words. "If you refuse to seek her out, the storm will only grow stronger and less manageable. You may come to a point where you are unable to control it when in her presence, or in the presence of anyone who upsets you."

"Yet, how does one apologize?"

"You simply ask for forgiveness. It is up to the other person to accept your apology or not, but if you do not offer it, it cannot be accepted."

He turned to her, his eyes pleading. "Yes, but *how*?"

She smiled up at him. "By simply saying you are sorry," she replied. "And always make an attempt to include for that which you are apologizing. Let me give you an example, if I may."

"Please."

"When I was a young child, my mother had a small porcelain bird she had received as a gift from my father. We did not have much, so that figurine had a place of honor on a small shelf my father had attached to the wall. One day, I was angry at my mother — I do not even remember why now — and in my anger, I slammed the door closed behind me. The force of the door being slammed closed made the bird fall to the floor, where it broke into a thousand pieces.

It could never be repaired. Apologizing for what I had done had not been an easy task, but I begged her forgiveness, and I made it clear that it was for my behavior that led to the breaking of her precious bird and not for the breaking itself. That is important. It was my behavior that led to the hurt; therefore, I apologized as such. My mother accepted my apology, and it gave me a wondrous sense of relief, for the guilt I felt had been great. It also brought a sense of warm pleasure by those actions."

"Did your mother replace the figurine?" the duke asked.

Emma shook her head. "No. She passed away the following year from a fever." It was easier to say the words now than in the past, but they still hurt.

"I am sorry about your mother."

"Thank you," she said. Then she turned back to look at him with narrowed eyes. "Yet that is not the same as giving an apology for a wrongdoing. Remember that."

"I will remember."

They stood looking out over the open expanse of hills without speaking, each in his or her own world until the duke spoke.

"I…am sorry for raising my voice to you," he said in a voice just above a whisper. "Forgive me."

"Of course, Your Grace," she said, surprised he would begin his apologies with her, a mere woman in his service. "There is no reason to apologize to me."

He turned to her. "There is. For if I do not, it is as you said; I risk the chance of losing you."

It was as if lightning had struck her. For a brief moment, she wondered if he meant to keep her by his side forever, but rational thinking returned. He spoke of their business arrangement and nothing more. What a fool she was. What was it about this man that had her thinking romantic thoughts? She simply could not understand any of it.

"Then, I forgive you," she said and was pleased to receive a smile in return. "May I ask you something?"

He gave her a nod as he looked back toward the hills. "You may."

"The anger that resides inside you?" she asked, doing her best to speak her words carefully. "Do you know its cause?

You do not have to share whatever it is with me, but it is important that you understand the underlying reason as to why you are easily upset."

She thought he would not respond for a moment, but then he sighed. "I do. Whenever it comes to mind, it makes my anger increase tenfold. I would say it is a curse. Would you agree?"

"If you allow it to control you, then yes, I could name it as such. It can also be a blessing."

He threw his head back and laughed, a clear, mocking tone. "A blessing?" he asked, still chuckling. "How could what makes me angry be a blessing?"

"It is a spark," Emma explained, ignoring his brusque behavior, "that could be used for good." When the duke scrunched his brow in confusion, she added, "Allow me to explain."

"Please do."

"When you find yourself angry, do not allow it to control you. Instead, use the energy it provides to guide you." She sighed in frustration, for her words were not making sense and she knew it. "The storm that rages there." She waved at the hillside toward the now dark clouds that had gathered.

"What of it?"

"The rain, the thunder, and the lightning all work together. They bring forth the rain that brings water for dry grass, to crops that thirst."

He stared off toward the coming storm for several moments before saying, "I have never considered it in that sense. So, you advise that I should use my anger for good?"

Emma smiled. "Indeed, Your Grace," she replied, glad her words finally were comprehensible. "When you find yourself angry, as you did with your friend, control the storm. Do not allow it to control you."

He shook his head. "But how do I do such a thing?"

"With practice," she said.

The duke drew in a deep breath and shook his head, but then his face took on a kind look.

"That smile is the answer."

"My smile?" he asked, touching his lips as if to feel the upturn of his lips.

"Indeed, for it is a very nice smile." Then an idea came to her. "Perhaps it is what you should practice. Every time you become angry, force yourself to smile."

This time when he laughed, it was filled with mirth rather than mockery. "Perhaps one day my name shall be Duke of Smiles rather than Duke of Storms."

This made Emma join in his laughter. "Perhaps." *And perhaps one day I will find a man like you, one who will take me in his arms and hold me,* she thought. Then her mind went off on its own again, bringing forth images of the two of them together.

That is, until he spoke again. "Today I have learned something new from you. I would like to visit my friend tonight and apologize."

"Of course, Your Grace," she said, wishing she could bury herself in a hole — or at least her great imagination, for all it seemed to do was cause her to suffer. "I must be on my way, as well."

"Will you return this week?" he asked as they began the trek back to the house. The first spits of rain began to fall, and they quickened their pace.

Emma wished to respond that, indeed, she would return. If it were up to her, she would never leave Bonehedge Estates. To make such a statement would be unfair to this man, for his heart was with another. Therefore, she replied, "I am afraid I will be very busy this week. Those new accounts and all."

"Oh." Was that disappointment she heard in his tone? But no, that could not be the case, for it made no sense. "Perhaps next Saturday?"

"I am sorry, but I have meetings all week." She hated to lie, but it was for the best. The closeness they shared, or at least the closeness she felt, could not continue, for one or both would be hurt in the end, and she could not take another blow.

"At night?" he asked in surprise as they stopped beneath the eaves of the house.

She sighed. "No, not at night." No lie would come to mind excusing her from an evening meeting with this man.

"Excellent!" he said with a wide grin. "I shall send my carriage for you at five Saturday next. You may join me for dinner."

Emma could do nothing but nod her agreement before the carriage rolled up in front of the house. A thousand thoughts swarmed in her mind, but only one returned to the surface time and again.

What kind of man had one woman on his arm and invited another to dinner?

Chapter Thirteen

Standing beneath the covered stoop outside the Babbitt home, Lucas swiped at the rain that covered his overcoat. The rain had held back its deluge until he stepped from the carriage, and he had not even had time to open an umbrella before water was running off the brim of his hat.

He considered the words Miss Barrington spoke earlier. Apologies never came easy for him, and when he had asked for forgiveness in the past, his motives had always been selfish. Perhaps they were now, as well, but regardless, he needed Ingrid's friendship, for he had few friends in this world.

He pounded on the door, and it opened to Osmond, Ingrid's young butler.

"Your Grace," the man said as he took a quick step back. "Please, come in out of the rain." He helped Lucas out of his coat and took his hat. "Lady Babbitt is in the drawing room. Would you like me to announce you?"

"That will not be necessary, Osmond," Lucas replied with a smile. "I know the way."

The man gave him a deep bow and moved to put away the dripping coat and hat Lucas had been wearing. Lucas then walked across the lavish foyer to the drawing room, admiring the manner in which Ingrid had redecorated in the Neo-Classic fashion favored by the *ton* at the moment. She had always been one to keep up with the latest styles, and her house reflected it.

He peeked through the drawing room door and spied Ingrid standing with a glass of wine peering through the window. It was not until that moment that he realized how important her friendship was to him. If she did not accept his apology, he would be devastated.

She turned from the window and gasped when she saw him. "Lucas?" she said, placing her hand against her breast. "What are you doing here?"

Lucas walked over to stand beside her. "I came to apologize," he said. "My actions when you were last in my home were uncalled for; in fact, they were horrible." He took her hand in his. "I am very sorry. I value our friendship more than you can imagine, and it is something I do not wish to lose."

"Your smile," she said in what appeared to be contemplation. "It is bright and addictive."

"My words, my actions, the accusations." He shook his head. "My temper," he added with a sigh. "You were correct when you said that I have allowed you to be the recipient of my anger, and you are the last person I wish to hurt."

"I know that," she said in a quiet tone. "It is why we are, and always will be, great friends, even in the worst of times."

Lucas was dumbfounded by her words. "Then you forgive me?" he asked in wonderment. "After I accused you of…" He cleared his throat, for the words were difficult to say. "Even after my accusations of trying to seduce me?" Hearing the words aloud made them all the more difficult to stomach, and he felt a complete fool for having thought them in the first place. Never had this woman made any attempt to be more than a friend.

Ingrid placed a hand on his cheek. "You are forgiven," she said.

As the words left her lips, a warmth filled Lucas, a calm and soothing feeling just as Miss Barrington had promised. Perhaps this new outlook on life would be worth the discomfort that preceded it after all.

"Would you like a drink?" Ingrid asked as she approached the liquor cart. "I have a new wine I would like you to try."

"Please," Lucas replied, although he continued to revel in the satisfaction of what had just taken place. He watched the storm as he waited, the windows vibrating lightly as the thunder rumbled through the air. The storm inside remained calm.

As a matter of fact, it was calmer than it had been in quite some time.

Ingrid handed him a glass of red wine and asked, "Now, will it be rude of me to presume a certain woman was in your company again today?"

He took a sip of the wine. "This is very good," he commented in surprise. "Where did you find it?"

"It was brought in from France just this morning. I placed a special order from a new vineyard I visited recently, and they did not disappoint." She gave him a coy smile. "And do not avoid my question."

He laughed. "I was not avoiding anything," he said. "And yes, Miss Barrington called in today, and we spent a small amount of time together." When she gave that same coy smile, he asked, "What do you think of her? I realize you only met her briefly, but you have always been a good judge of character. I promise I will not become angry."

She sighed. "Very well, I will give you my honest opinion," the woman replied. "Remember that you said it best; I have only met the woman for a very brief moment, so I judge based on what I have previously seen or experienced and not on anything I know of the woman herself."

"Go on, then. Tell me. I may not like it, but I will listen, nonetheless."

She walked over to one of the wing-backed chairs and offered him the other beside it. "I do not trust many people, but I especially do not trust those who are of the lower classes, not when it comes to matters of the heart. I mean, the woman is not even of the gentry, Lucas! I realize she has done you no harm thus far, and yet I cannot help but wonder."

"May I ask why? For I find her kind, beautiful, intelligent, so many qualities that those of the upper classes find appealing."

"It is because of those things," she said, turning toward him. "Lucas, you are a duke. It is expected you marry a woman who is of a titled family."

He could not help but see the truth in her words. "There are no marriage plans," he said with a laugh. "We are involved in business and nothing more, so there is no need to worry."

"Yet, I assume you have imagined the two of you as more? Am I right in assuming as much?" Before he could respond, she added, "There is no harm in that, mind you, and I must admit that since you have been in her company, you seem much happier and easier to be near."

Lucas raised his glass with a laugh. "What you say is true. I am amazed by her spirit and intrigued by her determination. I worry nothing about her intentions, for I believe them to be honorable."

"I worry about the rumors I have heard concerning her," Ingrid said. "Are you perhaps but another part of her scheme?"

"Scheme?" Lucas asked. "And what rumors? I have heard nothing concerning this woman."

Ingrid sighed. "Have you not heard that she has been to the home of Lord Miggs? It is said that she went to dine with him just last week."

His heart sank. It could not be true, could it? He had thought Miss Barrington attracted to him, but if she had her eye set on Lord Miggs, where did that leave him? Yet, if she was indeed in search of financial gain, would she not turn to a duke? Was she entertaining the baron in case Lucas did not come through for her? Of course, none of these questions made sense.

"I see by your expression you had not heard this rumor," Ingrid said with a sad smile. "She is poor, and her father's business is in ruins. From what I have heard, her father has not been seen in nearly a year."

Lucas nodded. "That much is true. She shared with me that her father has been busy attempting to secure more business for them out of London, although without much success."

"All the more reason to keep up your guard."

Lucas refused to believe such things of the kind woman who was helping him learn to control his temper. "Maybe she is conducting business with the baron, as well," he argued. "In fact, I can see no other way. She is much younger than he."

"Perhaps you are right," Ingrid replied with a shrug. Then she gave him a smile. "I do not say these things to cast the woman to the street. I just ask that you be careful, for you are young, handsome, and wealthy. You are a prize for any woman, even one such as myself."

Her smile was mischievous, and he could not help but feel the regret for his previous behavior return.

"Again, I am sorry for my accusation."

She laughed. "Think no more of it," she said. "Now, I do have some news that may disappoint you."

"Oh?"

"Lord Tritant has requested I attend the party Lord Gates will be giving at the end of the month." She placed a hand on Lucas's arm. "Now, I realize you already asked me, but would you be terribly hurt if I accepted Lord Tritant's invitation? I told him I would have to think about it before I came to a decision, but the truth of the matter is I wanted to be certain you would not mind."

"I see where this is going," Lucas said in mock suspicion. "You are requesting that I allow you to throw yourself into the arms of another." This brought on a bout of laughter, and when it ended, he added, "Of course, I relieve you of your promise to accompany me."

"You will still attend, will you not?" she asked, her concern clear on her face. "Please do not remain home on my account."

"Worry not, for I will attend. I promise. It will be good for me."

With relief, she moved the conversation to other matters, but Lucas considered the upcoming party. It was still two weeks away, and although Ingrid had warned him about Miss Barrington, he considered asking her if she would like to accompany him. The truth of the matter was he could no longer deny the feelings he had for her. She was the light he needed to push away the darkness he had inside him. In his heart, he knew they were meant to be together, and he would find a way to see that happened — the *ton* and their opinions on the matter be damned.

***

For the first time in his life, Lucas realized how empty Bonehedge Estate truly was. The guest rooms stood empty, the dining room was always quiet. The only sounds came from the servants as they went about their duties. The house could be filled. Filled with the laughter of Miss Barrington. Filled with her sweet voice driving away the storms in his life.

He pushed away his dinner plate, the outside storm that had arrived the day before increasing in intensity. He had overheard several of the servants whisper amongst themselves about bad omens, but he dismissed such senselessness. Omens were for those less educated, and he would not allow himself to fall into the trap of believing such drivel.

As he exited the dining room, he turned a corner and almost ran straight into Louise. The maid gasped, her eyes widening in fright before she moved her gaze to the folded sheets piled high in her arms. "I'm sorry, Your Grace," she whimpered. "I wasn't watching where I was going."

Images of the tongue-lashing he had dealt to this woman several weeks before rushed into his mind, and he could not help but feel sorry for the woman. She had always been a hard worker, and his treatment of her had been unfair. He would speak to Mrs. Flossum; there was no need for him to be involved with disciplining the maids any longer. That was the job of the housekeeper, and she was a strict, if not fair, woman he could trust.

"Louise," he said.

The woman looked up, and he could see the fear in her eyes. "Yes, Your Grace?" she replied in a shaky voice.

"Have I ever told you how much you are appreciated here?" She shook her head fearfully. "Then allow me to say so now. Since I was a child, you did your part to keep this home well-maintained, and I want to thank you for that."

Her eyes widened further before a smile broke out on her lips. "Thank you, Your Grace," she said, the fear now gone. "That means a lot that you'd say so."

"I am sorry," he said, and then remembered Emma's counsel, "for shouting at you before. I hope you can forgive me."

"I-I am but a servant in your house, not worthy of your apology."

Although her humbleness was great, it did not sit well with him. "You are mistaken, for even a duke who calls the sound of thunder must control the ability to call down lightning."

When her smile widened, he was shocked when that same warmth he had felt after apologizing to Ingrid filled him. What a wondrous feeling this was!

"Then I hold no grudge against you," the maid said and then quickly added, "not that I would've anyway, Your Grace." She bobbed a curtsy and moved to return to her duties, but Lucas called her back.

"One more thing. I shall increase your pay. Not as payment for the tone I used with you but rather in appreciation for your dedication to this household."

"Thank you, Your Grace," the woman said before hurrying away.

The relief that washed over him was like nothing he had ever felt in his life. The ability to seek forgiveness and receive it was new. And wonderful! How had it taken him so long to learn it?

As he entered the library, he picked up a candle holder and walked over to the single painting that hung from the wall over the mantle. His father gazed down at him, and for the first time, Lucas noticed the tiny frown that played at his father's lips. He studied that painting for some time as his mind wandered to the past.

How cruel his father had been to him, scolding him for every infraction. No matter what he did, Lucas could never please him. And as if a story unfolded before him, Lucas realized the true root of his anger. The hurt caused by his father had made him turn and lash out at those around him. It was a vicious cycle he now understood and, more importantly, would seek to end.

"You taught me much, Father," he whispered to the portrait, "yet you never understood the joy of forgiving another person. Or in listening to their tales." He sighed. "This lesson was taught to me by a woman who is not even of the gentry. A woman whose dreams are held together not by stitching but by hope." He could not stop his heart from swelling as he spoke of Miss Barrington. "I believe I might be in love with her."

The frown on the portrait seemed to indicate what his father thought about the matter. Perhaps he was correct; how could Lucas consider such a strong emotion for a woman he had only known for a short time? Yet, he could not shake it any more than he could have stopped the sun from rising on the eastern horizon. "Matters of the heart do not need your approval, nor that of Mother. The only opinions that matter are those of myself and Miss Barrington. I will seek only her approval; the rest do not matter."

As a sense of peace washed over him, Lucas turned to leave. He stopped and looked back at the portrait one more time. "You should smile more often," he told the painting. "Trust me, it does wonders for one's outlook on life."

Chapter Fourteen

Emma recorded the final sum in the account ledger and pushed it aside. She had not been as occupied as she had led the duke to believe, but more work had come thanks to Stephen's diligence. She had never been prouder of him, and today he agreed to travel two towns over in an attempt to secure more work. He was a quick learner, and although his reading and writing stills left much to be desired, he knew the correct terms to use to convince prospective clients he knew the business.

Her eyes fell to the next ledger, which belonged to Lord Miggs. Her stomach knotted as she thought on the arrangement she had made with him. Not only did she promise to dine with him, but he would also escort her to the party given by Lord and Lady Gates. Oh, how she regretted making such a commitment! Spending time with him was a chore in itself, and just the thought of it made her skin prickle. Granted, he had never made any attempt to put his hands on her, but she had seen that same look in his eyes as she had seen in the eyes of others. Lust. A stark contrast to what she saw when she looked into the duke's eyes.

Sighing, she leaned back in the chair. She was wasting her time thinking about a man who was well out of reach, but she found she could not erase him from her mind. He had apologized for losing his temper with her. The fact he had listened to her advice was astounding, yet that was not the only thing that kept him in her thoughts. The storm calming in his eyes had called to her heart, and her heart had wished to be in his arms.

"Stop!" she said aloud. He had a woman in his life. If she was to be any part of a man's life, she would not be his mistress! And no duke would marry a common woman such as herself.

"Then why does he invite me to dinner?" she asked the room. It was a riddle she had spent many hours reasoning out and still could not. Was it his plan to seduce her with fine drink? Perhaps he would begin to offer her jewelry. A flat. Fine clothes.

No. Although she knew it was possible, for anything was possible, but she did not believe he would do such a thing. She could see the goodness in him.

Perhaps it was his ego, having a woman to speak to when the duchess was not there. The guise of needing her there to work his books had long since passed. Yet, how strange it had been that he asked her to help him with his temper. She had done so to the best of her ability. Had she not given her word to do what she could to help?

Yet, doubt lingered. Perhaps the man was a rogue instead. She compared him to Lord Miggs for a moment. No, the two men were exact opposites one from the other. The eyes of the baron showed lust where those of the duke showed...something else she had yet to determine. Something good.

"It is because you have feelings for him," she whispered and then clamped her mouth shut. She scolded herself for thinking such a thing. As much as she tried to deny it, feelings for him did reside inside her. They were small, yet she could not deny they were growing. How could they not when she spent time with him strolling like a couple in love?

An image of Lady Babbitt popped into her mind once more. Although the woman seemed rude, or so Emma gathered from the short time she had been in her presence, she did not seem a lady who enjoyed sharing a man. This made Emma laugh. Did any woman enjoy sharing the man she loved? She doubted it rather highly.

Something had to be done about the duke. Although she enjoyed helping him and being in his company...*I definitely enjoy being in his company,* she thought with a smile. She had to dissolve this particular part of their agreement. She would continue to do his bookkeeping, but that work would have to be completed here in the office. She had to stay away from his home at all costs.

A woman could find herself in all sorts of trouble being alone with him there.

The door opened, and Emma gaped as the duke entered. His smile was radiant, and his eyes sparkled. His long hair was neatly tied back with a blue ribbon that matched his coat. She found breathing difficult as she stared at him. There was no denying it; she had feelings for him, an affection that would only lead to destruction and heartbreak if she did not put a stop to it, and soon.

"Miss Barrington," he said as he walked over to the desk. "I am glad you are here." He glanced at the ledgers. "I am not interrupting your work, am I?"

Emma could not help but notice the kindness in his tone, and without thinking, she responded "Not at all" before she could stop herself. Then she groaned inwardly. She was meant to break the ties that bound her to him! *Foolish girl!*

"Excellent," he replied. Then he paused before adding, "The storm outside has cleared, bringing about sunshine."

Emma walked over to the window. Good, they were discussing the weather. That was a safe topic of discussion with anyone. "Yes. Two days of sun. We are fortunate."

"We are."

An awkward silence followed, as if neither knew what to say, and Emma felt that familiar tightness in her stomach. It was torment being in his presence and feeling as she did. What she needed was to keep away from him.

"I must apologize, but I have work to complete," she said as she went to move past him to return to the chair behind her father's desk.

He placed a hand on her arm. "I must share something with you. A celebration of sorts. It is imperative I speak with you. But not here; some place private."

Emma glanced at the ledgers and receipts piled upon her desk. "I...my work..." She found the excuse on her tongue weak.

"An hour?" he pleaded. "Please, I will pay you for your time if need be. It is important." The sorrow, the need in his eyes stayed the protest.

"There is no need to pay me every time you speak with me," she said. "I suppose I could use a short break."

He released her arm and grinned. "I took your advice concerning apologies, and I was able to mend broken relationships. Come, let me tell you more about it."

She should have been happy he was able to mend his relationship with the woman for whom he cared, but she found doing so difficult. In her heart, she knew it was selfish to feel regret, so she took her own advice and forced a smile as she placed a cloak over her shoulders and tied the ribbon of her bonnet before following him out of the office. "I am glad," she lied. Well, it was only a half-lie, for she was happy he was able to take the steps he needed to better his life.

"I wish to tell you all about it," he said as he waited for her to lock the door to the office, although she had no idea why they could not speak there. When she turned, her concern grew when she noticed the looks of disapproval from those walking past.

The duke opened the door to a carriage, and she glanced around once more. "I am sorry, Your Grace," she said, "but where are we going?"

"You will see," he said, offering her his hand to help her enter the carriage.

"But the people," she said, looking around them again.

"What of them?"

"They will speak ill of you inviting a woman such as myself to ride with you in your carriage. You may throw me out if you must. Tell them I am your servant."

He laughed. "I would never do such a thing. And yes, I am breaking societal rules at the moment. The same people speak ill of me regardless of what I do. I care nothing for their whispers and gossip."

Emma sank back into the cushions, feeling defeated, as the vehicle picked up speed. There was no escaping the situation. Nor the smile that drew her in.

**

During the journey, they discussed the weather and business, but the subject of Lady Babbitt did not arise. Did he mean to take Emma to the woman? To flaunt the woman in front of her? Perhaps he meant to parade the love he had for Lady Babbitt in front of Emma to cause her to break down and cry. He had been cruel when he was angry; maybe she had misread his eyes and he was cruel always.

"Miss Barrington?" the duke asked, bringing her back from her silly thoughts. "Is everything all right?"

She went to nod, but when she glanced out the window, her heart froze. She had not paid attention to which direction they had gone, and now they were outside a familiar church. The grounds were meticulously kept, and large trees protected the dark-gray building from the elements.

"You look as if you have seen an apparition."

"No," Emma said in a choked voice. Did he know? How had he learned her secret? She had kept it safe from everyone bar Stephen. Did the duke bring her here in order to torment her? To show her he learned the truth? She would be ruined and forced to beg in the streets if that were the case.

"Shall we step out?" he asked, motioning to the open door.

Emma nodded, fear guiding her steps as she exited the vehicle. Although the storm had ended two days earlier, the wind that remained had a coolness to it.

The duke spoke to the driver before turning and offering Emma his arm. She took it with reluctance and followed him down the path.

"First," he said, "I appreciate you taking time from your busy schedule to meet with me."

"You are welcome," Emma managed to say, although she feared she would begin weeping if she did not get away soon. "May I ask why we are here?"

They walked around the side of the church and stopped beneath one of the great trees. Emma glanced around. For whom, or what, were they waiting?

"Lady Babbitt?" she asked.

"Yes?" Lucas replied with a scrunch of his brow. "What of her?"

"I do not see her."

He laughed. "That is because she is not here. I took your advice and spoke with her."

Emma was more confused than before. Nothing was making sense. "That is good," she mumbled. When he took her hands, she trembled. Although she enjoyed the feeling, she knew it was wrong. To be so intimate in such a sacred place was beneath any man, but more so when the man was a duke who had his eyes set on a viscountess.

"I explained to her what you have been teaching me," he said.

Emma nodded. What was the point of them coming here? The confusion became too great and the first tear rolled down her cheek before she could stop it.

"What is wrong? Have I somehow upset you?"

"I am happy for you," she whispered. "For both of you."

He stared at her, his face pinched in confusion. "Are you certain I have not upset you?"

"No, please, go on."

"Very well. I spoke to her just as you suggested, and she forgave me for my outburst! Is that not wonderful? And to think I lost my temper with her, and yet she continues to stand by me." He shook his head in disbelief.

"That is wonderful," Emma said. What she wished they could do was leave this place. Being so close to him with her traitorous feelings was difficult enough when they were not standing in front of a church.

"Yet it did not end there," he continued, clearly beside himself with excitement. "Louise, a woman who has been a maid in my home for many years and has never even asked for a day to herself? Well, not long ago, I had treated her badly, and I even apologized to her! I feel as if I am a whole new man!"

Although Emma was glad for him, she thought her heart would break. She did not want to be here — with this man, at this church — and panic threatened to choke the breath out of her. How could she not allow him to express his joy for what he had done? Therefore, she swallowed the panic and turned her attention back to the duke.

"The greatest part of this story?" he said, his eyes gleaming. "I went to the library where my father's portrait hangs, and there I realized something. I brought you here because this is the place of the first memory of my father scolding me. I had been playing under this very tree at the time."

A sense of relief washed over Emma. He was not here to call her out, to demand the truth. He was here to put behind him issues that had plagued him for years. "I am sorry to hear this," she said.

"But do you not see? I was hurt by his words, and in turn, I did the same to others. That was the realization to which I came! My anger over the years became so fierce that I called down lightning — using the words others have attributed to me — upon those who I felt wronged me. Even for the smallest infraction." He looked down at her and smiled. "Until I met you."

An uneasiness crept over her. "Your Grace," she began. She needed to stop him before they both made a grave mistake.

"Please, we are friends. Call me Lucas."

She stared at him for a moment. To call this man, a duke, by his Christian name was outrageous. Could she not do as he requested, especially a request as simple as this? "Very well," she agreed. "Lucas." It was easier to say than she had expected. "You seem to misunderstand something very important. I did nothing for you. The answers were inside you all along, and you found them. That was all you."

He chuckled. "You are too kind," he said. "Yet it was you, the very woman I threw out of my office and who came charging back in. That woman of strength, honesty, and integrity. A woman I admire greatly."

"I-I do not understand. I am none of those things." When he went to argue, she forestalled him. It was time to put an end to this charade. She had to sever the cord, as they say, for what they had would only be made into a mockery if his peers learned of it. Not to mention the blight it would put on her father's business. "Although I enjoy being in your company, I cannot do so any longer."

"But why?" he asked. "Have I hurt you in some way? I will make right whatever it is that I have done."

He attempted to take her hands in his again, but Emma pulled them away. "Please stop!" she cried. "This is not fair to Lady Babbitt!"

"Ingrid?"

"Yes. Your love."

He stared at her for a few moments before throwing his head back and laughing.

"Do you not respect her?" Emma demanded.

"Of course I respect her. You seem to mistake our relationship." He continued to chuckle as if it was all a great joke. "She is my friend and nothing more. You believed us to be courting? We are business partners, yes, and have been friends for many years, but I can assure you, we share nothing more."

Can it be true? she wondered. "There is something I am struggling to understand," she said aloud. "At your home, she spoke of me being a servant because of the way I was dressed. I thought she was jealous."

Lucas chuckled again. "When it comes to Ingrid, one never knows. She may have been jealous, but of you as a woman of beauty and strength. She worries for me, something I am learning friends do often. So, yes, she cares for me, but not in the way you believe."

Emma released the breath she had not realized she had been holding. Her fears had been unjust, and the smile he wore told her she had nothing about which to worry.

"I do not want you to leave my side, Emma."

His words shocked her despite the sweet melody they sung to her heart. Pain inside her broke away, and like a cool breeze, soothed her soul. He spoke highly of her, but she had lied to him. For some reason, a tugging in her heart told her she must tell him the truth. The confession could earn his ire and send her away brokenhearted. It could also ruin her completely. It needed to be told, for, eventually, he would learn it, and she did not wish to be mired too deeply to save herself when that moment came.

"Lucas," she said as she looked down at the hands that held hers. She turned to look at the small graveyard on the opposite side of the small iron fence beside them, the final resting place of those who had passed on into the next realm. "I am not all that I appear to be."

She gazed up at him and swallowed hard. The words needed to be spoken. "In fact, I believe before you say any more, I must tell you something very important."

"Of course," he said, concern written on his features. "What is it?"

"My father," she whispered.

"Yes? What about him?"

"He has not been traveling on business."

Chapter Fifteen

Emma walked beside Lucas, each step piercing her heart more. It seemed only fitting that a storm was gathering in the south, the dark clouds seeming to race toward them in order to oppress the air around them all the more. Emma had kept her secret close for long enough, and truth be told, she was exhausted. The lies and the weight of keeping the business her father had worked so hard to build from failing had become a burden she could no longer bear.

"I feel I have hurt you," Lucas said as they walked past a small row of headstones. "Perhaps this outing was not the best of ideas."

"You have done nothing," she replied. "You shared your heart, and now I wish to share mine." They came to the last row of headstones, and she led him to one that sat beside a stone wall. Although her heart was heavy, somehow, with Lucas at her side, she stopped before it. "Two years ago, my father suffered a stroke."

"I am sorry," Lucas said. "I truly am."

"At first, I thought he would recover, for he never gave up the fight." Tears welled up in her eyes, but she did nothing to stop them. "From his bed, he continued to work on the ledgers, or attempted to do so." She dabbed at her eyes with a kerchief Lucas offered her. "Thank you," she said and then continued. "As the days became weeks, he grew weaker. He lost the use of his hands, then his sight.."

Lucas held her hand, and she felt a comfort in his grip.

"At the same time, more business fell to the wayside, and I began to take over the books for him. He had taught me so much already, but I was overwhelmed.

Then came the hard times when people began to struggle. Barons, marquesses, even the butcher lost everything. Many lost their homes, fortunes vanished, debts increased, and even smaller businesses such as mine were left unpaid." She shook her head at the memories, for those had been terrible days indeed. "I found myself struggling to tend to both my father and the business. That is when Stephen came to my aid."

"Stephen," Lucas repeated. "Yes, your assistant."

"He is more than that; he is my dearest friend. He told me I was strong and that I would be able to help my father and keep his business from failing. He promised to stop drinking and help me." She laughed at the memory. "He slid back to his old ways only once in the beginning, but after that, he has never had a drink since, at least as far as I know." She sighed. "Last year..." Now the tears rushed down her face, and she allowed them to do so, for they cleansed her soul. "One day, my father never woke from his sleep."

Lucas pulled her against him, and for the first time, she wept. Oh, she had allowed tears to fall before, but she had always stifled them as quickly as they started. She knew that, once they began, she would struggle to stem their flow. Now, with her face pressed against his chest, she released the sorrow that had gathered behind the dam that kept her from falling apart for so long. And he held her close without saying anything until she was able to pull away in order to finish what remained of her confession.

"So, you see, I have been running his business, making excuses for his absence, all the while I have been tending to the ledgers myself in his name."

"I had no idea," he said. Thunder rumbled around them, but they ignored it. "I am terribly sorry for your loss and the pain you have been forced to carry."

She wiped away the tears with the kerchief. "I have tried so hard to keep this business going. And Stephen...he has done so well securing new accounts. For the first time in a long time, I believe the business will return to its former success."

"With you at the head of it, it surely will," Lucas said with a smile despite the light rain that began to fall upon them. "I only spoke with your father on a few occasions, but I know he would be proud of you."

He placed a finger under her chin and forced her to look up at him. "I know I am."

Emma found his words soothed her aching heart, but one more thing would ease her further. "You have helped me today," she said as she gazed up at him. "And learning from you, I will take your advice."

"How so?"

"I think I need to speak to my father."

He smiled down at her. "I understand. Take all the time you need. I will wait for you in the carriage."

"Thank you," she said.

He walked away and soon disappeared from sight. Emma looked back at the simple grave marking. There was so much to say, but she knew he had always preferred his conversations to be short.

"Father," she whispered as she knelt and brushed a leaf from the stone. "I believe in a short time, the business will once more be profitable." She pulled several weeds from the ground before her as she spoke. "Stephen has given up the drink, and I have met a very special man. You know him. Lucas Redstone. Yes, the Duke of Rainierd." She smiled and wiped tears from her eyes. "He makes me happy, Father, and I know I make him feel the same." She laughed as she imagined her father questioning her feelings for the duke.

"I know it has been a short time since I have known him. I cannot help but care for him. Do not worry, I am not going to marry him, at least not any time soon." She laughed again.

"Things have improved and they will only continue to get better with each day." She stood and gave the stone a final smile. "Thank you for showing me that which is strength, for it has guided me throughout my life."

With a sigh, she kissed her fingertips and then placed them on the top of the stone as the first spits of true rain began to fall. With a smile and a heart less heavy than when she arrived, Emma returned to the carriage.

***

Although rain from a dreary sky lashed against the window, Emma was anything but dreary. She had released a burden that had settled upon her heart, just as Lucas had done. As he sat across from her, he pretended to be enthralled by something outside the carriage window, but she had caught him glancing in her direction more than once.

"I wanted to thank you for allowing me to share with you," she said. "I feel a sense of relief. For sharing it and for you not using it against me."

"Never," he replied. "My father had been adamant that women knew nothing of business, and I must admit that I had believed the same at one time." There was a twinkle in his eye. "Now I know better."

Heat warmed her cheeks and she wondered if it was possible to feel such strong feelings in such a short amount of time. Her friend, Heather, had met a man for whom she professed her love the very next day. At the time, Emma had thought it ridiculous, but now, she found she understood her friend's feelings.

The carriage came to a stop in front of the shop. She knew it was time for her to leave, but one thing plagued her mind. "Earlier, you mentioned something about us. Did you have something more you wished to tell me?"

"I did," Lucas replied with a small smile. "I believe it might be best to wait until our dinner on Saturday. We have both had an emotional day."

He was right. Her emotions were tangled, and time to organize her thoughts — and perhaps a nap — was in order. "Thank you," she whispered. "For everything." She leaned over and kissed his cheek. "I will see you on Saturday."

"I look forward to it," he replied. When she went to alight from the carriage, he caught her by the arm. "I think there is a lot more we can share with one another. For now, I want to thank you for all you have done for me, as well."

As he smiled, Emma noticed lightning flash behind him in the distance. It was only a week earlier when she thought that a sign of his anger, something that brought her fear. Now, it brought about a new feeling, one of hope and, dare she say, love?

"Goodbye," she said and then signaled to the waiting driver to open the door. Stepping out, she let out a laugh as the rain immediately soaked her dress. She rushed to the door, turning to wave before going inside.

What a change today had been. Business was increasing, the duke had learned how to keep his ledgers — and his temper — under control, and for the first time in her life, Emma was contemplating love. It was a beautiful feeling, a marvelous feeling. She wished she had someone with whom she could share this wondrous news, but all of her friends were married and had moved away.

When she opened the door to the office, she stepped inside. Stephen sat at the desk with a ledger in his hands. Although he could not read, he played his part well.

"Miss Emma?" he asked, placing the book on the desk and rushing to her. "Are you all right?"

She laughed. "I have never been better. In fact, I believe I am in love!"

Chapter Sixteen

Saturday was upon Emma before she knew it, and she had set aside the pile of ledgers earlier than usual in order to ready herself for the evening. The pale blue dress with its intricate lace around the neckline and tiny flowers embroidered across the bodice had been her mother's, and the thought of it stored away in a trunk made her want to weep. It was with great happiness when she donned it that it had fit her perfectly; no need to let it out or bring it in. To share such characteristics with her mother was a pleasure, for it kept the memory of the woman alive.

Her hair had not been as simple to address. It took her several attempts at putting it in place in an intricate chignon before she gave up and simply pinned it back and left two curls hanging down on either side of her face. How women of the *ton* wore such complicated styles, she did not know, but having a lady's maid most certainly made all the difference in the world.

The perfume she applied had been given to her by her father three years earlier. She had saved it for special occasions, and what could be more special than an invitation to dinner with the man one loved?

With one last look in the mirror, she affirmed that she was as ready as she would ever be and made her way down the narrow staircase that connected her private living quarters, as tiny as they were, with the office below. Sitting in his usual seat was Stephen, who jumped up when she entered the room, his eyes wide and his smile great.

"Well, what do you think?" she asked, lifting her skirts and turning around. "Do you think the duke will like it?"

"Oh, Miss Emma," he said, "if any man doesn't recognize your beauty, he's a fool."

Emma giggled. "You are too kind," she said, giving him a small kiss on his stubbly cheek. Then she glanced at the clock on the wall and sighed. "I suppose I am not very good at this dressing for dinner thing; I still have an hour to wait before the carriage comes to retrieve me."

Before Stephen could respond, a rap came to the door. Emma peered out the window and saw the outline of a carriage waiting. "It seems Lucas has no patience, either. But an hour early? He must be mad!" Despite her words, she giggled at the thought that she had been ready despite the fact he had sent the carriage early.

It felt as if she was floating upon the clouds as she opened the door, but then she frowned. This driver did not belong to Lucas.

"Miss Emma Barrington?" the man asked.

"Yes, I am she."

"I am your driver," he said. "Are you ready?"

"Oh, yes, I am," she replied, though she wondered what had happened to Walburg. The driver had been a kind man with a bright smile, though he was getting up there in years. Perhaps he had retired, and this man was his replacement. It was not as if Lucas kept Emma informed on what staff he retained or released. "Let me just get my wrap."

Once her wrap was settled on her shoulders, she gave Stephen a quick hug. "Wish me luck," she whispered in his ear.

"It will be perfect. And don't you worry about the office. I'll be here in case new clients come calling."

"Thank you," she replied, suppressing a giggle. What clients would come calling after dark on a Saturday? She shook her head. He did all he could to be helpful, and in all honesty, she could not have survived without him.

"I am ready," she said when she reached the door. The driver bowed to her before helping her into the carriage — she almost giggled again; having someone bow to her was not something to which she was accustomed — and soon the carriage was trundling down the street.

Emma leaned back into the cushions. She did not realize Lucas had more than one carriage, but he was a duke after all. More than likely he had several. She closed her eyes and allowed her mind to wander. Perhaps after their dinner, they would take a stroll through his gardens again. There they would share their hearts and he would take her hands into his. As they gazed into each other's eyes, they would profess their love for one another. How deeply those feelings ran inside Lucas, she did not know, but she suspected they were like hers; that is to say, they were great.

Then she imagined him leaning in and kissing her. Would it be a gentle kiss, one of caution? One so soft she would float away? No, for his strong hands would hold her in place. Perhaps it would be a kiss of passion, one of urgency.

Regardless of the type of kiss, it would be the first of many, and as their love for each other grew, one day he would ask for her hand in marriage. Of course, she would accept. They would have a gaggle of children and share a loving home.

She would have to give up keeping the books in order to mind the children, but other bookkeepers could take up that task. A duchess did not do such things, did she? One thing was certain. Stephen would take the room upstairs above the shop and remain on the payroll assisting the new manager. She would see to that.

She had been so lost in her thoughts that, when the carriage came to a stop and she opened her eyes, she stared in shock at what was not the grand house of Bonehedge Estate but rather the home of Lord Miggs.

***

Fear knotted Emma's stomach as she was led through the foyer and into the drawing room. The baron stood near a single bookcase, his silver hair pushed forward as was the style for many of the *ton* these days. His large stomach pressed against the well-tailored coat, and the lace on his heavily starched shirt stood straight up, grazing his chin.

"Ah, Miss Barrington," he said in a voice that echoed in the room. He spoke as if the room was filled with people, but when she glanced around, they were the only ones there. "I thought you might have declined my previous offer," he said.

Emma, finally coming around to herself, dropped into a curtsy. "My lord—?" she went to ask but stopped when he raised a hand at her.

The baron approached her, and his gaze made her uneasy as he looked her up and down. His reddened eyes and the strong odor of liquor told her that he had already had much to drink.

"Such a beautiful creature," he whispered. "Tonight shall be a splendid evening."

"I believe there must have been a mistake," Emma said.

The man laughed. "A mistake? How so?"

"Forgive me, but I already have an engagement this evening. I had thought the carriage that came for me was—" She cut her words short with the flaring of his nostrils.

"From another gentleman?" he asked.

Emma nodded, fear gripping her as tightly as if it were his hands around her throat.

Lord Miggs snorted. "I see." He walked over to a small table and placed his glass upon it, his back to her. He said nothing for several moments, and Emma wondered what she had done wrong.

"My lord, perhaps we can meet on another evening." She did not want to offend this man, for he would not hesitate to throw her into the streets, rent paid or not. "We could—"

"There is no need to explain," he said, his back still to her and his tone sharp enough it could have cut her in half. "You may leave."

She stood in stunned silence. His words were what she wanted to hear, but she had not expected them to come so easily. Her uneasiness had her curtsying again, although he could not see her do so. "Thank you, my lord," she said. "I promise that next time—"

"There will be no next time." He turned around, and Emma could not help but take a step back from the fire that roared in his eyes. "You have embarrassed me, and although I should force you to walk home, I will remain a gentleman by keeping my promise to have my driver return you to your home."

"Your promise?"

He came to stand before her. "Indeed," he said and then let out a laugh. "I recall an agreement for dinner and then escorting me to a certain party. In return, your rent would remain the same and I would continue doing business with you...or rather your father."

Emma stared at Lord Miggs as the realization of his words settled on her. "I do not mean to break the promise I made to you. I was not aware you had returned—"

"Whether or not you leave is your choice." He studied her for a moment. "This gentleman friend of yours? He is of some...interest?"

"He is," she replied in a whisper. What business was it of his to ask such a question? She was not in a position to argue with him, not a baron, and certainly not the man to whom she paid her rent.

"Here is what you must know," he said as he glared down at her. "Go to him, break your promise to me, and I wish you no harm in life." A grin spread across his face, an evil grin that brought a shiver to Emma's spine. "If you do so, our arrangement will be forfeit." He took a hefty drink from his glass. "Or remain here as my guest tonight per our agreement, and I will do as I promised."

He brushed a finger across her cheek, his touch cold and unpleasant, making Emma's stomach tumble and churn. Everything inside her screamed to run, to go to Lucas and tell him what had transpired. As the baron let out a heavy sigh, worry gripped her. She needed the baron's account, and he was her landlord. To upset him now just as she was getting the business out of debt would ruin her.

As his eyes bored into hers, she reached up and touched her cheek, expecting to feel a scar left behind by his caress.

"This is purely a business arrangement, correct?" she asked in a near whisper.

"Of course," he replied as if his intentions should have been clear. He pulled his hand behind his back. "I am but an old man in need of the company of a lovely young woman. You have nothing to fear."

She thought on his words. In all honesty, she had no other option than to agree. She still did not have the money for the past rent, for, although she had gained new clients, it would take a month at the soonest to receive payment. If spending a few hours with the baron kept him at bay in turn, she would do so. Lucas would understand.

Offering Lord Miggs her best smile, she replied, "Thank you, my lord, I will stay."

"Good," he replied with a wide grin. "It is the best decision you could have made."

Chapter Seventeen

T he storm Lucas had kept so well under control simmered in the back of his mind as Walburg stood before him.

"I'm sorry, Your Grace," the driver said, "She wasn't there. A man named Stephen said she had left an hour before, but he was as confused as I."

Lucas released a heavy sigh as he shook his head. None of this was making sense! If she had left an hour earlier, she would have been at Bonehedge Estate already. And why would she hire her own carriage when she knew he was sending one for her. "Did Stephen say where she went?"

"No, Your Grace," Walburg said, visibly shaking. "He thought it was your carriage that collected her."

"Did the man say anything else?" The driver seemed to hesitate, and Lucas glared at him. "Speak, man! This is important!"

"He asked me if I need, or knew anyone who needed a bookkeeper," Walburg said. "Promised the best rates and services."

Lucas snorted and dismissed the driver. He had learned what he would from the man. Walking over to the cabinet, he took out a bottle of brandy and poured himself a measure.

Something was not right, yet he could not place it. The manner in which Emma had looked at him, how she had shared such intimate details of her life with him at the church. Revealing the secret of her father's passing had to have been difficult. Not only because she had lost her father but because Lucas was an important client.

Tonight was meant to be wonderful, for he had meant to share his feelings for her. He would have fulfilled any request she made; no cost was too high.

Then an unsettling feeling coursed through him as rain began to dance against the window. Was she with another man? And if so, to what purpose? He shook his head in an attempt to dismiss the thoughts, but it did no good. Rather than dissipating, they solidified and became clearer, and no matter how hard he tried, he could not rid himself of them. Images of her in the arms of a faceless man as he held her close and kissed her. Of her dancing with him. Of her in his bed. With each image, his rage grew, and when Goodard came to the door and asked if dinner should be held, Lucas had to control his tone.

"I do not believe that will be necessary," he replied. "It appears Emma has chosen another over me this evening."

"Are you certain?" the old butler asked.

"I see no other possibility. Another carriage collected her, and I cannot see any other reason for her absence."

Goodard took the now empty glass from Lucas's hand and refilled it. "Your Grace, if I may offer my advice?"

"Please," Lucas replied. "For I feel that my temper may get the best of me, and soon."

"I have seen the manner in which Miss Barrington looks at Your Grace. Although I do not know the woman well, perhaps a great emergency has sent her away. I do not believe she would do anything to upset you purposefully."

Lucas took a sip of his brandy and thought over the man's words. "Perhaps you are right," he said with a sigh. "I will eat now. I hope she sends word as to why she did not come, and then I can learn the truth."

"As you wish," the butler replied.

Lucas made his way to the dining room and took a seat at the table. He closed his eyes and listened to the drumming of the rain on the window. Emma must have had a good reason for not joining him for dinner, but no reasonable explanation came to mind.

The more he turned it over in his mind, the stronger the storm inside him became, and if he was not careful, it would match the one that raged outside his home.

***

Three times Emma thought the baron had made an attempt to kiss her. The first was when he had helped her remove her wrap. His mouth had come dangerously close to her ear, and she covered her shock by commenting on and walking over to a vase that sat on one of the nearby tables, although she found it gaudy and out of place.

The second had come when he showed her a rare coin he had acquired at some point Emma could not remember. As she pretended interest in the coin, he had moved in to point out what he said was the head of Caesar Augustus, although she saw nothing of the sort. To her, it appeared more a peacock than a human head, but what did she know of coins? In her shock, she dropped the coin and used that as an excuse to move away from him in order to retrieve it.

The third suspected attempt had been when he insisted on pulling out her chair at the dining table. She had shied away when he had leaned in to retrieve the napkin she had not seen fall to the floor.

She was not able to ease the tension in her shoulders until the man was safely in his chair at the head of the table, far enough away she did not have to worry he would overstep his bounds. Why she suspected such a violation on her person, she did not know, but simply being in the company of the man made her uncomfortable.

By the end of dinner, the tension was gone. The baron proved to be a good conversationalist, had read many books on various subjects that Emma found interesting, and had seemed interested in her opinions on a variety of matters. When he invited her to see his library, far away from the ears of the servants, concern returned, but to her surprise, he only boasted of his books and did nothing that would have been thought as inappropriate. Perhaps she had misjudged this man after all.

"One more glass of sherry before you leave," he insisted as he took her empty glass from her. She was not accustomed to alcohol, and the room was already moving on its own accord, but she did not protest. "I have bottles brought back from France twice a year. The French may not have much in the way of manners, but when it comes to liquor, they do produce the best."

"I would not know, my lord," Emma replied. "What we have had tonight has been very nice." She accepted the new glass from him. "Thank you for your kindness."

He smiled at her, but this time, rather than the pleasant grin she had seen him wear throughout dinner, this smile seemed devilish. "I am kind," he replied. "It is why I have decided to inform you now of a surprise I meant to keep from you."

"A surprise?" Emma asked suspiciously. "What sort of surprise?"

"Allow me to show you," he said.

Her heart seized as his cold, bony hand clamped around hers. Rain pounded on the windows, although she could barely hear it over the pounding behind her ears. As they walked, fear constricted her breathing. What a fool she was! He was leading her to his bedroom where no one would hear her cries, and if they did, they would be servants who would do nothing in order to keep their positions in his household.

Rather than going up the stairs that led to the second floor, he walked past them and into his study. "You look frightened," he said with amusement.

"Not at all," Emma said, glad her voice did not shake, although her legs did. Thank the heavens for skirts! "I believe the wine has dulled my senses somewhat."

His eyes flickered for a brief moment, and Emma thought she saw a hint of evil in them. No, that could not be, for he had been nothing but kind and generous all evening. Despite this fact, she could not stop the feeling of impending doom that settled on her. Yet, that was silly; she had misjudged him several times. As an old man, perhaps having a young woman to dinner and being able to boast about his books made him happy.

"Good," he said. "This is your surprise." He patted a stack of letters, perhaps six in total, that sat on a table.

"Forgive me, my lord. I do not understand."

The baron laughed, and lightning flashed behind him, increasing that uneasy feeling she wore like a cloak. "Before I left for my trip, I sent out letters to ten men of wealth. I informed them of your business, or rather, your father's business."

Emma smiled. What a kind thing for him to do.

"Of the ten, six have replied with great interest in securing a bookkeeper. They shall also be in attendance at the ball Lord and Lady Gates will be giving in two weeks' time."

Relief washed over Emma, as did regret for her suspicions. "I cannot thank you enough for your kindness," she said. If she could secure those accounts, her business would be out of debt within the month, two at most. She could finally purchase her new dress and perhaps new furniture for the office.

"Like most men," the baron said, reaching for her hand again, "these men are not enthused to do business with a woman."

Emma felt her heart sink.

"I shall tell them we are courting. This will only be an act, of course," he assured her. "I suspect it will be enough to gain their confidence. I believe it will bring you the business you need and therefore you will be able to pay what you owe me. Do you not agree?"

"It will," she said in a near whisper, referring to the accounts and not his proposal of courting. Once the words left her lips, she realized her mistake too late.

"I would like you to come to dinner again on Friday," he said.

The last thing Emma wanted was to spend too much time with him. "I would love to, but—"

"Excellent!" he said before she could object. "I believe a nice partridge is in order. I will inform the cook once you have left." He raised his glass, and Emma forced herself to do the same. As the storm outside raged, she wondered at the same storm of worry that brewed inside her.

Chapter Eighteen

E mma entered the office of the business that had once belonged to her father more confused than any time in her life. Her mind was in such a muddle, she was unsure what agreement she and the baron had made.

Lord Miggs had continued his conversation about their supposed courting, and she had done nothing to ask for clarification because she had been under such a confused fog, thinking had been difficult. He had spoken as if the courtship was more than a sham, and now that her head was clearing, she hoped she had not agreed to something more.

She traced a finger across the old wooden desk, and the answer came to her almost immediately. It was for the business she had agreed to that sham. The business her father had begun but now was hers. She had no intention of failing, and if the cost was high to maintain it, then so be it.

Yet, how high was too high? That question she was unable to answer.

She poured herself a glass of wine and thought about the agreement they had made. Arriving at the ball on the arm of the baron would elevate her to the *ton*. She had already agreed to accompany him, therefore that had not changed.

What had changed was how others would view their relationship. Now, rather than an accompanied guest, she would be something more. What would the *ton* think of her, the daughter of a bookkeeper who had never owned a ballgown in her life, being courted by a baron?

Lord Miggs did not seem to care or he would never have made such an agreement.

It was not the baron's wealth she coveted. If every one of the six men allowed her father's business to take on the keeping of their books, she would have a respectable income, and it had been a long time since that had been the case.

She walked over to the large window that looked outside. Large puddles had formed along the edges of the footpath, and in the street rolled heavy streams of water. Would this rain never end? Would any of these storms — those that whipped up the wind and poured down rain as well as those that sent her life into turmoil — would any of them end?

How many times had Lord Miggs made to appear he would take advantage of her? Had all that been in her imagination? Yet, he had used his books and the coins he collected as ways to impress her instead. How had a man such as he remained such a gentleman? That was where her confusion lay, for it mattered not what the man owned; her heart was with Lucas.

Lucas. She would call to his home first thing in the morning and explain what had kept her away. Once she had settled everything with him, she would collect Stephen and the two would return to the baron's home in order to clarify their agreement. She could not have him believing there was more to their relationship than he thought. If her words angered him, she would simply explain that she would still accompany him to the ball but not as more than his guest. Courtship was reserved for Lucas alone.

The door flew open, hitting the wall with a great bang, causing Emma to yelp in surprise. The cold wind blew papers off the desk, and she rushed to close it only to encounter a dark figure in the doorway. Lighting flashed behind him, but she could just make out the face of the Duke of Rainierd. And he did not look happy.

Emma took two steps back as Lucas entered the room. Water dripped from his hat and cloak, forming pools of water at his feet, but Emma only glanced at them.

"Lucas!" she said with a gasp. Then she smiled. "I am so glad you are here. I must apologize for this evening. You see—"

"Quiet!" he said. He did not shout, but the whispered word made her take in a great breath as if he had shouted. With a kick of his heel, he slammed the door shut behind him. "You were with a man this evening. Who was it?"

"It was a business meeting," she said. "One I had—"

"His name." The tone struck down her back like a whip.

"Baron Miggs, a man who—"

"You have seen before?"

Emma started. "I do not know what you mean by your words, but if you are assuming—"

"Did you not go to his home before?" He took a step forward as he glared down at her. "Do not lie to me!"

"Lucas, your temper, please," she said, although the words were choked.

He narrowed his eyes at her. "Do not insult me. With how many men of the *ton* do you spend time?"

The glass Emma held slipped from her hand and shattered on the floor. The duke paid it no mind as it crunched under his boots. "Tell me!" he said through clenched teeth.

"I have met with Lord Miggs twice," she replied as she brought a hand to her breast in an attempt to place some sort of protection between the man who glared down at her and herself. It was a feeble attempt, but it was all she had.

"Who else?"

"There have been no others, besides yourself, of course. I can assure you, it is not as it appears!"

The laugh he gave held no mirth. "Oh, I know how it appears," he said. He looked her up and down. "It appears in a cheap dress. It appears with a smile and promises of better days."

"Lucas, please," she pleaded, but he ignored her.

"And it appears as though you have taken me for a fool."

Emma could do nothing to stem the tears that fell down her cheeks.

"Do not speak to me again," he seethed. "Nor even mention my name. I was warned about your tricks, and now I see them for what they are!" Then he turned, stalked to the door, and placed his hand on the handle.

"No!" She ran after him and caught his arm before he could leave.

"I had no choice!" she wailed. "I had to do what I could to save the business! To save my home!"

Lucas stopped and turned, his face obscured by the shadow of his hat. "There are names for women such as yourself," he said in a low tone. "But I am too much a gentleman to speak of such things." Then he walked out of the room, the door slamming to punctuate his harsh words.

The tears increased as Emma lowered herself to the floor. Wrapping her arms around her knees, she wept. She wept almost as hard as she did the day her father died, for her heart had broken once more. Outside, the storm continued to rage. At the start of the day, there had been sunshine, a day so bright she thought it a sign of her future. Now, lightning flashed and thunder exploded, a sign that only dark days loomed ahead.

***

"There now," Stephen said, handing Emma a cup of tea. "That'll make you feel better. My mother used to make me one when I wasn't feeling well." He draped a blanket over her shoulders, and she gave him a small smile of thanks.

Emma had not slept more than an hour, and Stephen had found her on the floor by the door where she had fallen asleep after weeping throughout most of the night. He had led her straight to her bed, started the fire, and put on the kettle before pulling a chair near and asking her what had happened. As the water heated, she told him all that had transpired the night before.

"I am unsure as to what to do," she said before taking a sip of the hot tea, its effects calming. "His temper was so great, he refused to listen, and I dare say, I doubt he will ever wish to listen again."

Stephen frowned. "I should go to his house and let him know what a scoundrel he is!" he said, balling his hand into a fist. "You are too good for the likes of him, Miss Emma. I'm sure of that! You don't need his account now that we've had so many new ones come in."

She gave him a grateful smile. "I am afraid I have ruined everything," she sighed. "I care nothing for his accounts; it is the man for whom I care. I…we were growing close." She wiped at her eyes. "I am sorry."

"No need to apologize to me," he said, producing a well-worn kerchief and leaning over to hand it to her. "You tried to tell him the truth, didn't you?"

"I did," she whispered, her mind replaying the events of the previous night in her mind. The duke had spoken over her, much like the thunder that roared outside. "He refused to listen."

Stephen shook his head. "Men are like that." Emma giggled, but he did not seem to notice as he began to scratch his head. "Makes you wonder if most of us have pudding for brains." He continued with his thoughtful head-scratching for several more moments before sitting straight up in his chair and giving her the widest smile Emma had ever seen. "Yep, we don't listen too well, do we?"

This time Emma did laugh.

"Are you all right, Miss Emma?" he asked, concern etched on his face.

"I am better," she replied, waving off his attempts to cover her with the blanket once more. "Thank you so much."

With reddened cheeks, Stephen nodded and refilled her teacup. "Well, at least that storm has gone," he said with a grin. "The sun is shining down on us again."

Emma smiled. The room had no window, but she could see light glowing between the cracks of a few bricks where a window had once been. If only it was indeed a sign of good things to come, but Emma doubted very highly it was the case.

"I must speak with Lord Miggs when I go to his home for dinner. We must clarify our arrangement." She heaved a heavy sigh, wishing she could retain the calmness that had fallen upon them. "I fear he will be unhappy with what I have to say, yet it must be said."

Stephen scratched behind his ear. "Don't forget your appointment with Mr. Montgomery at four on Friday," he said.

Emma groaned. "I did forget." What would she do now? She doubted Lord Miggs would be willing to change their dinner to another evening, or a later time for that matter. How had she gotten herself into this mess?

"Could you just write him a letter?" Stephen offered.

"No. It would be best if I spoke with him in person." She threw the blanket aside; the heat from the fire had made the room stifling hot.

"Now, what do I do concerning the duke?"

"Men just need time to let their tempers settle," Stephen counseled. "Give the man a few days, and then go talk to him. He should've calmed himself down by then."

Emma gave an unladylike snort. "I doubt he will be wishing to speak to me," she said. "In fact, I know he will not. I am not sure what to do about him."

"Let me help. I have an idea that'll help both you and the business."

She turned from the kettle she had placed over the fire once more. "And what is that?"

"It's simple," Stephen said as he returned the chair to its place at the small eating table she rarely used. "Come Friday, if you haven't heard from him, I'll return his ledgers saying there's a mistake. Then I'll tell him that not hearing what you have to say is the big mistake; one he'll never forget." He raised his chin and gave a stiff nod to punctuate his words.

Emma was so overwhelmed with emotion she almost began crying again. Rather than weeping, she hurried over and wrapped her arms around Stephen. "I am truly grateful for your friendship," she whispered in his ear. "Thank you! I think that is a magnificent idea!" She kissed his cheek, and when she stepped away, the poor man blushed as he scratched his chin, clearly confused about how he should feel, and Emma giggled.

"What's so funny?" he asked.

"Everything," she replied as he gave her another confused look.

Chapter Nineteen

Lucas paced the library, his temper growing tenfold with each passing he made before the fireplace. Days had passed since his encounter with Emma, and a part of him wished to see her again. To be in her calming presence, for it was what he needed. A larger part inside him counseled that doing so would make him a greater fool than he already had proven himself to be.

He glanced up at the portrait of his father, the disappointment clear on the man's face. "You were right, Father," he said, clenching his fist. "You said I would one day be fooled by a simple woman, and it happened. I thought I would prove you wrong, but I fell into the trap she set. If only..."

He could not finish the thought, for he still cared for Emma. He had planned the perfect dinner for her, a night of celebration for his defeat over his temper and for the romance that had blossomed between them. Yet, what had transpired had been a mockery, a farce that left him the biggest fool of the century.

Then he thought of the warning Ingrid had given him. Like his father's advice, he had dismissed hers as much as he had dismissed the woman herself. The rumors concerning Emma had been true, for Emma had admitted her involvement with Lord Miggs.

Lord Miggs? What would she see in such a man? He was much older than she, a widower who was rumored to have lost his wife by her own hand. A man whose stomach grew with each passing year.

"Your Grace?"

Lucas turned to find Goodard at the door.

The butler gave him a diffident bow. "Your ledgers have arrived, and the gentleman wishes to speak with you."

"Who?" Lucas asked.

"A Mr. Stephen Foreman."

Lucas sighed. "Send him in."

Emma's assistant still wore the same coat Lucas had seen him wearing the previous two times they had met. Although it was cheaply made, he stood tall and proud as if it had cost ten times the amount he probably paid for it.

"Your Grace," he said, bowing over two ledgers he held in his arms. "I have come to deliver the ledgers you left behind."

Was this the reason the man wished to be brought to him when all he had to do was leave the books with Goodard?

"Set them on the table," Lucas said, pointing to a small oak table by the door. "You may go. Your presence is not needed here."

"Well," the man said as he shifted on his feet, "you see, there's been a costly mistake done, Your Grace. One that'll cost you a small fortune."

Lucas eyed the man. "What do you mean? I have gone over these ledgers several times, and there are no mistakes." To prove his point, he picked up one and scanned the entries. Each was written with a clear hand, and he could not see any errors.

"The vast wealth is Miss Emma," Stephen said. "That's the treasure you don't want to lose."

Lucas slammed the book shut and tossed it on the table. "I will not have an old drunk chastise me!" he said through a clenched jaw. The man cowered before him, but Lucas did not care. Let the old fool be afraid; it was only what he deserved for his outlandish attempt to get at Lucas. "Who do you think you are? Have you been drinking? Surely you are drunk!"

Stephen gave him an indignant look. "I'm not drunk, Your Grace. Far from it. Miss Emma says I'm a gentleman now." He jutted his chin forward proudly.

Lucas laughed and then glared at the half-wit. "You may not be drunk at the moment, but I can assure you that you are not better than the man you once were. A man who cannot read, wears a three-pence suit, and believes he has a part in society is an idiot." He gave another mocking laugh. "No, you are no gentleman, I assure you, no matter what coat you wear or what Miss Barrington says."

To his astonishment, the old man stood up straighter and nodded. "I might be all those things, Your Grace, and even more. But Miss Emma showed me mercy when no one else would. She tells me every day how fortunate she is to have me as a friend." He wiped at his eyes without embarrassment for the tears that he wept. "But you see, a gentleman — or a duke or even a cobbler — knows in his heart that he's the lucky one to call her a friend."

Lucas pushed down the pang of guilt that rose inside him. This man, this drunk, dared to speak to him in such a manner? "Never speak to me again!" he shouted at him, his words vaulting forward with the force of his anger. "Get out of my house, or I shall have you taken by the magistrates!"

Stephen took a step back into a chair behind him, moved around it and bumped into a table, almost overturning a vase that sat upon it. Then he turned and hurried out of the room.

Grabbing the ledgers from the small table, Lucas threw them across the room, his echoing scream reverberating off the walls.

***

Emma stood in the doorway to the office as the sun sat on the horizon. Other shopkeepers had closed their doors for the evening, and few people remained in the street. Most of the people had gone home to waiting families, where they would share in food and laughter. Whether their home was a magnificent castle or a simple cottage, they shared one thing; they all had someone with whom they could share their heart.

How Emma wished she had as much. It was strange that a short time ago she had thought she would have that with Lucas. Her feelings for the man had blossomed much faster than she would have ever anticipated, and she had longed for them to explore where their relationship might lead. Now, it had all been whisked away like a goodwife sweeping away the dirt on a floor. Had her dreams been wild fantasies with no hope of coming true?

"Miss Emma," Stephen said as he walked up to her. Gone now were his smile and the pride he wore with his new coat. Even the light swagger he had adopted had disappeared. As he drew near, Emma could see his news even before he spoke. "I'm afraid I failed you." He pushed a fist into his opposite palm. "I told the man he's a fool! That he should realize that he's going to lose you." He sighed. "His temper is even worse now, and he wouldn't listen. I'm sorry."

The despondent look he wore tore at what little was left of Emma's heart. She placed a hand on his shoulder. "It is not your fault; it is mine."

Stephen gaped at her. "Don't say that," he said. "You've not done a single thing wrong. He's the one at fault, not you. I know you care for him, but I tell you, he's not worth a farthing of caring!"

Emma blinked back a tear. "Stephen," she said in a low voice, "everyone is worth being cared for. It is why you helped me, is it not?"

He scrunched his brow. "Well—"

"And I helped you, did I not?" she continued. "Even when others thought you were not worth their time?"

He gave a sad nod. "You did, and I'll always be grateful."

"The duke is consumed by anger, much like you were once consumed by spirits. You know how it can destroy you."

Stephen sighed. "More than I care to admit. I guess everyone deserves a chance. Even dukes who are cruel."

"Yes," Emma said as she walked over to the window and watched the last rays of sun steep the horizon in pinks and oranges. "We have a future ahead of us regardless of what the duke has decided. I am thankful for having you as a friend in my life. If I could, I would tell everyone what a wonderful man you are."

"I?" Stephen asked in surprise. "I don't deserve recognition. I failed you today."

The sorrow in the eyes of the older man tore at Emma, and although she was heartbroken from the rejection of Lucas, she had to keep the world around her shining brightly.

"You have not failed me," she assured him. "You set out to complete a task — to deliver a message to the duke — and you did just that. If he did not care to listen, then that is beyond your control."

Stephen studied her for a moment. "I like the way you think," he said with a wide grin. "So, what's the plan now?"

"We shall continue forward as we have," she replied. "I am to meet with the baron for dinner on Friday. We are to discuss business, but I would like to also clarify a few points of our agreement." Just the idea of pretending he was courting her made her stomach churn. "After I have secured more accounts, I believe not only will we be out of debt, but I shall be able to give you an increase in your wages."

"You'll never have to pay me," Stephen insisted. "The kindness you've shown me is more than enough as far as I'm concerned." He looked down at the floor. "I know the duke hurt your heart, and it's the worst kind of hurt anyone can have. But I believe there's a gentleman out there who'll appreciate you for who you are."

"Thank you," Emma said as she leaned in and kissed his cheek. The poor man tried to hide his blush by turning away, but Emma had seen it quite clearly. He truly was a dear man.

When Stephen had left for home, and Emma had poured herself a glass of wine, she gazed out the window. Stars twinkled in the sky as her mind thought on Lucas, the pain in her heart still fresh. He had taken wondrous steps to control his temper, but now it consumed him. Despite his anger, she could not help but have a great affection for him, and she suspected that would remain the case for some time.

Stephen had said that, somewhere in the many villages that dotted the English countryside, a man existed who would appreciate her for the person she was. As she looked out upon the now-empty street, she could not help but cling to the hope that the man of whom Stephen spoke was Lucas.

Chapter Twenty

Emma was thankful when the time she was to have dinner with the baron had arrived, although the days waiting had been excruciating. The finer points of their agreement had to be clarified before it was too late. She looked forward to ending that madness and then moving on to securing the new accounts he had promised.

The idea excited her. In just over two weeks, she would have enough funds to pay up the rent she owed, thus appeasing the baron and hopefully beginning a new future. A small part of her worried the baron would be angry, for she had seen the lust in his eyes. He looked at her as some sort of prize he had won, but she was no such thing. Her heart belonged to one man, and that was certainly not the baron.

She had sent Stephen home early, and now, as she was wont to do, she watched people as they strolled down the footpath. It was a particular habit she had, but it was also a game. As she observed the various people, she would attempt to guess about who they were. What types of relationships did they have? What occupations? Where might they be going? And why? It was all a bit silly, if she was truly honest with herself, but she found the game took her mind off whatever was bothering her at the time.

A couple strolled past, and the woman glanced in Emma's direction, her eyes going wide. She spoke to the man beside her and entered the office.

"Emma!" the woman said with clear glee. "I cannot believe it is you!" She hurried over and gave Emma a hug.

"Susan, it is so good to see you," Emma replied, kissing the cheek of the woman who had been a friend from long ago. "How are you? And how is Ephraim?"

Her friend waved a hand in the air. "Oh, he is busy most days, but that does not matter. I have money to spend on new dresses and activities to keep me busy." She looked Emma up and down, and the tiniest of grimaces appeared on the corner of her lips. It was gone so quickly, Emma was not certain she had seen it.

Rather than concern herself, Emma smiled. Susan spoke the truth about her own success. The dress she wore was beautiful, far nicer than anything Emma had ever owned. Regardless, Emma was pleased her friend had married well and was happy in her new life.

Sadness filled her when Susan glanced around the office in apparent distaste. "How is your father?"

The question caught Emma off-guard for a moment. "He is well." She regretted lying to her friend, but if even one more person learned the truth, she would never keep any of the accounts she had. "I am helping him with the bookkeeping and enjoying doing so."

"You were always the one who found such things entertaining," Susan said with a shake to her head. She reached out and took Emma's hand. "I must ask you something."

Alarm filled Emma, but she could not understand why. She and Susan had been longtime friends and had shared the most intimate of secrets of how they would each marry a man of courage and wealth.

"Why did you choose to become a spinster?" Susan asked. "You realize it is why we cannot be seen with you nor invite you to parties, do you not?"

"We?"

Susan sighed. "The old friends such as Hannah and Rebeca. While we chose to court, you chose to bury your nose in ledgers. It is a bit off-putting, you know?"

There were many things Emma wished to tell the woman whose parents spent every pence they had on assuring their daughter was presentable to men who had money. Although Susan's parents had some wealth, they had struggled just as many others had.

Now, she seemed to have forgotten what life was like for those of the lower class, and Emma could not deny the hurt she felt over the arrogance and judgment she saw in her former friend.

"I am sorry you view me as off-putting," Emma said, removing her hands from Susan's. "Some things are beyond my control, but—" She stopped when a carriage pulled up in front of the office.

Susan turned back to Emma. "So, the rumors are true. I know that carriage and driver. You are keeping company with the Baron Miggs."

"I am," Emma replied, feeling her defenses rise. "It is only business I am conducting with him and nothing more."

The once kind-hearted girl who had cried on Emma's shoulder over the cruelty of her mother's words no longer existed, for in her place stood a woman who wore a smirk of distaste.

The door opened, and Susan's husband pushed his head inside. "Susan dear, I am growing impatient with waiting." He did not even look Emma's way, and Emma felt another wave of sadness rush over her. He had always treated her kindly in the past, but now he held his nose high and ignored her outright.

"Goodbye, Emma," Susan said. "It is unfortunate that you have resorted to such ways. Ephraim warned me, but I did not listen. Now I know better." Then she turned and glided out of the office.

Anger and shame overwhelmed Emma, though it should not have. Susan had never lifted a finger in order to help another, and yet she felt she could judge Emma? Why did no one understand that she was doing everything she could to save her father's business?

As a matter of fact, why did anyone feel the need to concern themselves anyway?

***

During the carriage ride to the home of Lord Miggs, Emma had rehearsed what she would say to the baron. In her mind, she explained to him her concerns and he readily agreed. All she could do was hope that what happened in reality was as simple.

Dinner had come and gone, and still she had not broached the topic. As she accepted a glass of sherry from him as they sat in the drawing room, she knew she could put it off no longer. Emma had wished to sit in one of the large wing back chairs, but the baron had insisted she sit beside him on the plush couch. He sat a respectable distance from her, for which she was relieved, and he continued to refill the liquid in her glass whenever it became low.

"Dinner was splendid," Emma said, ignoring the lingering eyes of the man beside her. "I wish to thank you again for the business we have conducted together."

"Of course," the baron replied. "In a week's time, we, or that is you, will have more business."

He reached over and patted her leg, and Emma thought her dinner would rise. His hand did not linger, so she attempted to ignore the intimate touch.

"Yes, about that," Emma said. The baron reached once more for the decanter of sherry, and she said, "Oh, no thank you. I really should not have more."

"Oh, but you will," he said with a laugh as he refilled her glass. "As you were saying?"

Emma sighed. She had to build up her courage to be straightforward with what she needed, but it was not easy. Rumors had already spread about her and this man, and accompanying him to the party under the guise of courtship would only make matters worse.

"The new accounts you are helping me secure. I am indebted to you and thank you for all you have done."

The baron arched an eyebrow, clearly hearing that she was not overly pleased. "I must admit I am concerned with telling people we are courting."

Lord Miggs sighed. "And why is that?"

"As it is, my lord, I find it distasteful to lie to others. I also am concerned that it will give the wrong impression. Do you not worry that saying such a thing would prevent a lady who seeks your attention from finding it? That would be unfair to her."

Rather than be angry, as Emma had expected, he gave a mirthless laugh. "Each time we meet, my generosity increases," he said as if annoyed. "And yet, there is always more demands made by you.

It seems I give and you take."

Emma stared at the baron in shock. How could he believe such a thing? "My lord, that is not what I meant to do."

"And yet, that is what you do." He placed his glass on the table with a loud clink. "So, now I shall treat you as you treat me."

Emma went to take a sip of her brandy as she attempted to find the words to calm him. Before she could drink, he grabbed the glass from her hand and set it beside his.

"My lord?" she asked in surprise. "I am sorry. I did not mean to offend."

He narrowed his eyes at her. "Your act of innocence must come to an end," he sneered. "I have been nothing but kind to you, and in exchange, I receive cruelty. I find it quite unfair of you."

Dread filled Emma. Now she would lose his account as well as the ones she might have secured the following week. That, combined with the account she lost with Lucas, meant that her life was now over.

"I know about your father."

Emma widened her eyes. "Excuse me?" she asked as her heart beat against her chest.

The baron gave an evil grin. "He has been dead a year, has he not?"

Emma's mind raced as she tried to ascertain if he knew or if he was attempting to get her to admit what he had guessed. He gave her little time to decide, for he added, "I have known for several months now. Burying the man two villages away was not a smart action on your part."

Emma had never felt such fear in her life. This had gone well past worrying about what others thought of her and the baron together. To learn her father had died and that it was she who kept the books would only result in all her clients leaving. "My lord, I did not want people to think—"

"That a woman was overseeing their books?" he asked with amusement. "That a woman, as most women are prone to gossip, may tell others of their financial standing?"

"I would never do that!" Emma said indignantly. How dare he make such an accusation of her!

"Perhaps you would not, but the people will now know the truth."

His grin would have been comfortable on a man convicted of murder. "For I shall tell them."

As he rose from the couch, panic raced through Emma. "No, my lord! You cannot!" She reached for his arm, and he glanced down at her hand in disgust. "Please! I beg of you. I cannot pay rent as it is! And my accounts are few. If word was to get out about my father, I would lose it all...my business, my home. Everything." How strong she felt in times past to be able to hold back her emotions, but those days had hope. Now, she imagined being left to live in the streets with nowhere to go.

"Ah, so you have returned to beg for my mercy, have you?" he asked. It was with great reluctance she nodded. "The woman who changes her mind and agreements with each meeting and demands even more from me believes she deserves mercy?"

"I will do anything you wish!" she cried. "Please, all I ask is that you do not tell anyone my secret."

The baron looked down at her and then reached into his coat pocket to produce several notes. "You will buy a decent dress," he said. "I cannot have the woman I am courting appearing in clothes such as what you are wearing now, can I?"

Emma had little choice. The cat had caught the mouse, and with his claws thoroughly sunk into her, she had to do as he requested.

"Now, pick up your sherry," Lord Miggs said. "We have much to discuss." He retook his seat. "For I will be your new business partner."

"I beg your pardon?" Emma asked as she stared at him.

"Do you believe I am going to allow you to keep all the money from the accounts I have given you?" he asked with a sinister smile. "No. From this point forward, you and I own your business together."

Chapter Twenty-One

The days that passed were a miserable lot, and with dark clouds hanging over him, Lucas pondered his future. Had anything truly changed since he learned the truth about Emma? In all reality, it had not. He still had work to complete, and that kept him busy enough to make him forget about the woman who had taken hold of his heart. Unfortunately, the times when he was not otherwise occupied brought about the fiasco that had torn her away from him.

A week earlier, Stephen had come by in some feeble attempt to make Lucas 'see reason' as he put it. That had been irritating enough in itself, but he had also had the audacity to call Lucas a fool. A fool! How dare an old drunk who had done nothing with his life call a man of title, a duke, no less, a fool! Lucas should have seen him dragged outside and whipped to an inch of his life for such words!

Yet, Lucas found he could not, for what Stephen had said was true. Emma was a treasure in so many ways. Her beauty, her insight, her outstanding abilities in so many areas, all of it had captured him, and he felt great affection for her because of those things. Yet, he had mistakenly trusted her with his heart, and in that, perhaps he was a fool. He had been a simpleton to believe he could tame a woman with such beauty and strength.

"How on Earth did that idiot of a baron tame her?" he whispered.

"Beg yer pardon, Your Grace?"

Lucas looked up. One of the gardeners — he could not recall his name at the moment — gawked at him as if Lucas was some sort of circus performer. "You fool!" Lucas shouted as he pointed at a perfect rose lying on the ground beside the man's boot. "I do not pay you to trim the actual roses! Even a child knows this." It was a minor infraction but for some reason Lucas felt hot rage coursing through his veins. "I shall dock you a week's wages for this! Now, if you wish to keep your position, I would suggest you keep your eyes on your work and not on what I am doing!"

The man gave Lucas a trembling bow. "I'm sorry, Yer Grace. It won't happen again."

Lucas gave him one last glare. "See that it doesn't." Then he continued his trek down the cobbled path. He had hoped getting a breath of heaven would help calm his nerves, but it appeared not even a garden stroll would give him any relief. How was it his temper had worsened since that nasty encounter with Emma? Perhaps it was because he was meant to be an angry man. Pent up anger had to be released somehow. Yes, that explained his current state perfectly.

He came to stand at the far gate that looked over the rolling green hills with which Emma had been so fascinated. How he missed sharing the magnificent view with her. Her words had been so soothing and calming, like a salve on a horrible wound. Now, he ached again, and it was as if his wound had festered now that she was not beside him.

On the horizon, clouds darker than those above him gathered. How was it he could have thought the storm gone for good? For now they had returned with a vengeance. The fault was his. Had he not treated Emma horribly? Perhaps he should have given the woman her say. Yet, it was too late for that now; the damage was done, and too much time had passed. Besides, she had found happiness with Lord Miggs. That was not something Lucas could easily forgive.

"Your mood grows dark like a winter's night."

Lucas started and turned to see Ingrid approach, her emerald-green dress accentuating the green flecks in her eyes. "What are you doing here?" he asked. Why could people not simply leave him alone?

"You do not wish to be in my company?" she asked as she came to stand beside him. "Perhaps you would rather brood alone."

He gave a heavy sigh. "I find myself full of regret."

Ingrid gave a sniff. "That is nothing new, Lucas," she said. "Is it this woman, Emma, for who you feel regret?"

He spun to glare at her. "Are the tongues of my servants so loose that their words have traveled to your estate?"

She shook her head and pulled her wrap in closer as the wind increased. "Not at all. A friend who ignores invitations to dinner does so for a reason." She reached out and placed her hand on his arm. "You cannot allow her to destroy you."

"That is the problem," he said as he turned to stare off at the stormy clouds that continued to roll toward the estate. "I must admit, I cared for her deeply." He snorted. "I still do. It is I who is destroying myself, not her."

"You still feel for her even after you learned she cares for another?" Ingrid asked in a shocked tone. She slipped her arm through his. "Come. Let us stroll."

With reluctance, he led her down one of the small paths, but he would not be rushed. He needed time to think before returning to the work that awaited him in his study.

"You are a good man, Lucas Redstone," Ingrid said as if speaking of what they would be eating for dinner. "One who is kind — when his temper is not raging, that is." She shot him a smile, but he ignored it. She sighed. "You are a friend who is valued."

Lucas stopped short. "Like a treasure," he mumbled as the words Stephen spoke of Emma came to mind.

"Indeed," she replied. "You are hurt, and rightly so. To simply leave with another man when she had promised to meet with you was not only rude, but unforgivable. I will say this with care, for I know you still have feelings for her—"

Lucas placed a hand on that of his friend. "Please," he said. "What is it you wish to share?"

"The truth of the matter is she is not a member of society. For a duke to court a woman not even of the gentry is unheard of, and I feared you would be ridiculed for such an act. Therefore, is it not for the best that she has found another man in whom she can sink her claws?"

"I suppose you might be right."

She laughed. "Suppose I might be right? My dear friend, you know I am right. She is a spinster who has become desperate; a woman so desperate she has to play games in order to get what she desires. I fear you are not the first, nor will you be the last."

As he listened, Lucas realized that some of what Ingrid said was true. One thing bothered him. "Do you not do the same?" he asked.

Ingrid laughed again. "All women do," she replied. "Yet, there are ways to do such a thing, some more civilized than others. For example, having a handsome man escort her around his property is a more civilized manner to gain the attention of men."

This made Lucas chuckle.

"Now, that is better seeing you smile."

Lucas thought his heart would soar into the sky as he recalled Emma speaking the same words. As the wind increased around them, the anger and fog from his mind took wing. It had been Emma who had stood up to him when he was angry. It was she who had spoken to him about his temper and shared her own struggles. Had she not confided in him about her father? Perhaps, as Ingrid had said, she had played games in order to gain something, yet it was only fair to understand why she had done so. Was it because of the loss of her father? Or perhaps jealousy over other women. Regardless of her reasons, maybe he could advise her as she had him. He could help her see the error of her ways, just as she had done for him.

"Tonight, I will go to the ball," he said as they continued their stroll, a new hope rising inside him. "Tomorrow, I will call on Emma and listen to what she has to say."

Ingrid stopped and turned to him, her features filled with concern. "Oh, Lucas, I fear you will only sink further into heartbreak if you were to do such a thing. Do you honestly believe it is worth it?"

Lucas thought of Emma, of her smile and her strength. The manner in which she made him feel, her words always encouraging, and he knew the answer. It was time he returned the favor.

"Yes, she is most definitely worth it."

***

The gown was the color of the sea with intricate lace around the neckline and at the edges of the puffed sleeves. Tiny white pearls created intricate patterns on the bodice, and a white bow lay just beneath her breasts. The garment exposed more bosom than Emma would have preferred, but the woman at the shop assured her it was of the latest fashion, so Emma had accepted the advice given to her. What did Emma know about the latest fashions? Yet, as she gazed at her reflection in the mirror, Emma could not feel anything other than regret.

It was not that the dress was not beautiful, for it was. Nor was her despondency due to the fact that her hair or the light makeup she had applied did not work well, for they did. No, her dejection came from the fact that, somehow along the way, she had ruined everything.

She had allowed the baron to blackmail her, allowed him to not only take control of her business, but now her life. He had spoken at length of his plans for her future. He made suggestions that were more demands about how she would run her business and the stakes he would take. With Lucas no longer speaking to her, she now had no one to whom she could turn, no place to where she could escape. The dress had been the nail on the coffin, for she had wished to make this first purchase on her own, with her own money. And she had wished to bring a smile to Lucas's face and not lust to the baron's eyes.

It was too late for regrets. She had made her bed, and therefore, she had no one to blame but herself for lying in it.

The wind whistled through tiny spaces she never could find in order to cover them, so she grabbed her cloak and made her way down the stairs to the office. The weather had not let up for days, and Emma had become accustomed to seeing the dreariness around her. Perhaps the sun would be gone forever and storms were to be her life from this day forth. After all that had happened, she could not see the world in any other light.

Her thoughts turned to Lucas as she waited for the baron to arrive. Lord Miggs had been adamant that she be ready on time, so she made certain she was early in case he decided on time was too late. He had always blustered, but his rancor had deepened, and she could take no chances. She hated to be forced to depend on him, but without Lucas, what choice did she have?

Lucas was such a different man from the person she was, and despite their differences, they had made a connection of sorts. She hoped that, one day, he would allow her to share with him what was on her heart. More than anything, she wished to tell him she loved him. To what extent that love was, she did not know, for experiencing such an emotion was new to her. The question was, would she ever be relieved of that feeling? In her heart, she knew she would not. To imagine loving another was unthinkable, for her heart belonged to him, and denying this truth was pure folly.

One fear that gripped her was for the man himself. If he continued on his current course, would his anger one day consume him much like a storm consumes a fishing boat upon the sea? She prayed he would find a way to calm it, for if he did not, he would sink beneath the crashing waves of his temper as quickly as that boat.

Turning, she walked over to the desk and ran a gloved hand across the old wood. She closed her eyes, and memories of her father sitting hunched over the various ledgers came to mind. When she was young, he would hug her and place her upon his knee as he told tales of dukes and viscounts, promising her that, one day, a man of title would fall in love with her, so much so that he would do anything she requested. Although she knew Lucas was wealthy, she cared nothing for his money or the fine dresses it could buy. No, all she wanted from him was his love.

The door behind her opened, and she shivered in the cool air that filled the room. In the doorway stood Lord Miggs.

"Let us go. The ball will begin soon, and I will not be late."

Emma nodded. Then she tapped the desk with her hand, perhaps for a sign of good luck. It was not that she believed in such nonsense, but she would need whatever help she could get. When she had locked the door, the baron grabbed her elbow just as the first droplets of rain came down.

"Tonight will be wonderful," he said with a wide grin that did not reach his eyes. "All of my friends will see the fine catch I have made."

Sadness filled Emma as she stepped into the carriage, and the feeling increased when Lord Miggs sat beside rather than across from her. He placed his arm across the back of the seat, and Emma held her breath, certain he would lay his arm across her shoulders.

He glanced down and licked his lips. "Did you wish to say something?" he asked. "I can ask the driver to stop and allow you to alight so you can return to your office alone if you would like."

The man had no idea how tempting his offer was, even if it meant being seen left in the now pouring rain to walk back alone after dark. "No, my lord," Emma whispered. "I wish to remain with you." How the lie grated on her! She had little choice in the matter. If she wanted to save her father's flailing business — no, her flailing business — she would have to remain beside this horrid man.

"As I thought," Lord Miggs replied with another of his grins that sent a shiver down her back and made the hairs on the back of her neck rise. As the carriage continued its journey through the muddy streets, he did not remove his arm from the back of the seat. Nor his eyes from her bosom. And Emma could do nothing but stare out the carriage window, wishing it was Lucas sitting beside her.

Chapter Twenty-Two

The estate of Lord Wesley Gates was a grand structure with large spires and high ceilings. The ballroom was not as large as the one at Bonehedge Estate, but it rivaled even the greatest of mansions in the area. Large chandeliers sparkled much like the fine crystal glass Emma held, although she took little interest in the wine within it. She and Lord Miggs had arrived an hour earlier, and upon her first look at the stately room, she could not help but feel a bit intimidated.

How could someone of her class be allowed to enter such a place? The people who milled around her were nothing more than people, even if they were wealthy. They ate, drank, talked, and danced; although, their manner in conducting themselves was more reserved than those who attended parties of the lower class. How could anyone be so stiff?

She made every attempt not to stare at the jewelry the women wore around their necks and on their fingers and ears. The amount of money that went toward purchasing such trinkets was more than she would ever make in her lifetime, and yet these women wore them as if they were nothing. Their dresses and gowns had been crafted by expert hands, much like the one she wore, and their hair was set in the latest styles. The men stood beside them in fine coats, their laughter drowning out the sounds of the men and women playing instruments in the corner.

"I have business to which I must attend," the baron whispered in her ear. "Do not do anything to embarrass me or ruin any opportunities I seek for you. As a matter of fact, I believe it would be wise if you would sit down in one of those chairs. Remember, you and I are courting, which means you are to decline any requests for dances."

"Yes, my lord," Emma replied with a sigh, repulsed by the man but thankful he was willing to leave her alone. It was doubtful any man would request a dance, and she was happy to deny them even if they did. If he believed he was hurting her, he could not have been more wrong. The only thing that brought a damper on her current situation was the realization she could not leave without his permission. Otherwise, sitting where no one would bother her was much better than forcing her to be at his side at all times.

She stopped to take a glass of wine from the refreshment table before taking a seat along one wall. Lightning streaked across the sky, and she watched it through one of the large windows that ran alongside the wall beside her. Smiling politely at the men and women who moved past her, she cared not that they did not return her greetings. Let them live their dispassionate lives; hers was null anyway.

As the conversations around her melded together into a buzz, she considered what she had done to her life. Here she was, a spinster made to appease an older man in order to continue with her business. Yet, was it worth it? This was the problem that continued to gnaw at her heart and mind. With the new accounts Stephen had acquired for her, she was certain she could do it on her own, but the rent she owed made that impossible.

It was as if she were in a deep hole, and the harder she attempted to climb out of it, the more of the sides fell in on top of her. If she could reach the top, she would be free. She could not reach the top without the help of the baron, not if she did not wish to be thrown out into the streets. Although, at times she could not help but consider that it was a more desirable place to be than in the company of such a vile man.

It was what he would ask for later that gripped her insides. He would not be happy to simply have her on his arm while they attended parties together.

No, eventually he would want her in his bed, and the thought made the liquid in her glass slosh as her hands trembled at the idea.

Seconds turned to minutes, and another hour passed. Emma wished Lord Miggs would return, for the stares she received increased, and her discomfiture worsened. Then her heart skipped a beat as a small group of people not five paces from her laughed, their attention drawn to one man: Lucas Redstone. How had she missed his entrance?

The fact he was there made her heart palpitate. He was as handsome as ever, his long hair pulled back and tied in a ribbon at the nape of his neck. His black coat contrasted with the bright white of the lace on his shirt and perfectly tied cravat.

Then his gaze met hers as lightning flashed outside and thunder rattled the windowpanes, and his smile faded. She held her breath as he walked toward her.

"Emma," he said with the slightest bend of his neck. "May I ask you something?"

"Anything," she said, the words barely able to leave her choking throat. How she wished to fall into his arms, to tell him of her worries, and to ask that he take her away from here!

"The rumors of the baron? Are they true?" His eyes held hers, and she could not help but see the pain behind them.

Before she was able to respond, the voice of Lord Miggs boomed through the room, much like the thunder that proceeded it. "Your Grace," he said as if seeing Lucas was the most marvelous thing to happen to him in recent days, "what an honor to see you here tonight."

Lucas nodded his greeting but made no reply.

"I do hope that my Emma has not disturbed you."

"Your Emma?" Lucas asked, attempting to hide his astonishment and clearly unable to do so.

"Why yes," Lord Miggs replied with that wide grin of his. "Miss Barrington and I are courting. Had you not heard? We are also conducting a bit of business together, but that is of little consequence."

Emma wished to scream when Lucas gazed down at her, to tell him that she had been cornered into the agreement. She felt more the mouse than she had before, for her lips would not speak the words. What if he did not believe her? She would simply upset both men, and she would be left with nothing. No, she would keep silent.

Lucas gave her a polite smile. "I was just going to say how much her dress is admired by a dear friend of mine."

Emma glanced over at Lady Babbitt in her green dress, who had her gaze fixed on Emma.

"Oh, yes," the baron replied. "I bought it for her. Speaking of business, why do we not speak of such things later; if you wish, of course."

"I am afraid I am quite busy, but perhaps another time."

In a moment of courage, Emma stood and went to speak, but he turned and walked away to join his group of friends, one who was smiling at him in much the same way Emma herself had on more than one occasion.

"He is not worth my time," Lord Miggs hissed as he watched the man walk away. "Come. It is time you met some of your new clients."

With heavy steps, Emma followed the baron, yet her heart and eyes returned to Lucas. If only she could turn time back to a fortnight ago. She would tell him exactly how she felt, and then perhaps they would not be where they were this night, which was to say, apart.

***

As the storm outside intensified, so did the rage grow inside Lucas. Somehow, he had hoped that the rumors he had heard concerning Emma and Lord Miggs were untrue, that the only arrangement the two shared were related to business and nothing more.

That was not to be the case, for the proud smile the baron presented and the new gown Emma wore — she could not have purchased such an article of clothing herself — these two things told him all he needed to know: he had lost the woman forever.

How he could lose such a prize to Lord Miggs baffled Lucas. Baffled and enraged him. He found himself wondering why she would choose such a man over him.

The only answer that made sense was that what Ingrid had said was true; Emma was looking for a man of wealth to marry her. There was no other way to see it.

Despite this truth, he could not help but study the woman from across the room. She had been left to sit alone in a chair, reminding Lucas of a child being disciplined. The baron was off with other men drinking and laughing, a common scene at events such as this.

To leave such a woman alone for other men to approach was not common, not when she was spoken for, and Lucas wondered at the wisdom of such a man. More than one man had, in fact, approached Emma, but she had denied them all. Was there more to their relationship than what could be seen on the surface?

Lucas debated whether it would be prudent to speak to Emma once more, but deep down, he knew it was futile. He could not deny the feelings he had for her, but images of his father flashed through his mind, the man chastising Lucas for being weak.

"Those who are empathetic to others are the weakest," he was wont to say. "For once you feel sorry for some 'troubled soul', you are pulled into whatever game he is playing. Then there is no one to blame but yourself for whatever losses you incur."

Despite his father's counsel, Lucas could not help but feel a sense of loss.

"The wine flows as freely as the gossip, and yet you remain alone," Ingrid said as she came to stand beside Lucas.

He looked at her and then at the other guests. What she said was true; he had no doubt that what they shared now with gusto had been promised to be kept secret not an hour earlier.

"I remember now why I never left my home in the past," Lucas said before taking a hefty drink from his glass. "Balls, parties, weddings, dinners. They are all the same, are they not?"

"Intrigue me," Ingrid requested with a raised eyebrow.

"I find I enjoy being around few of these people," Lucas explained. "The ones I do are already…otherwise occupied." He looked at Emma as he spoke, and Ingrid seemed to follow his gaze.

"I will not tell you what you already know," she said. Then she grabbed his arm. "Come. Join me and converse with the masses."

Although he wished to be left alone to wallow in his own self-pity, he sighed and followed his friend. Perhaps the distraction of a conversation would help keep his mind off Emma. As they moved through the crowd, Lucas asked, "And Lord Tritant? Where is he this evening?"

"Oh, he is off conducting some sort of business with Lord Miggs," Ingrid replied of the man in whom she had taken some interest. "Apparently, the baron has joined forces with your Miss Barrington as her new partner."

"Yes, I heard the same," Lucas replied. "And Lord Townsend? Has he caused you any problems?"

Ingrid laughed. "None whatsoever. When I told him I was not interested, he turned his interests to Miss Henrietta Donovan. She seems smitten with him, and she is welcome to him, I say."

Lucas chuckled, but he found it difficult to concentrate on anything other than Emma. Something nagged at him. Emma had stated she was nearly out of debt, and yet she had taken on a business partner? And Lord Miggs to boot? She had a better business mind than to do such a thing. That was not what had him worried. She had also agreed to allow him to court her, if the rumors were correct. If the former made little sense, the latter was incomprehensible.

His doubts were interrupted, when Ingrid introduced him to a couple with whom she had a mild acquaintance. The conversation they had was polite, yet brief and boring. He found it difficult to keep his mind from returning to Emma, for the troublesome thoughts continued to plague him. He turned to where Emma sat alone in her chair, and when he brought his attention back to those around him, the couple was gone.

"Lucas," Ingrid whispered, her voice filled with concern. "You must go to her."

"I cannot."

Lord Tritant walked up and gave Lucas a nod. "Your Grace," he said with a smile, "forgive my rudeness, but may I speak with the viscountess for a moment?"

"Of course," Lucas replied, glad for a moment of reprieve to deliberate the grand puzzle that made up this newfound relationship Emma and Lord Miggs shared.

The more he thought on this riddle, the greater became his anger, and the more he realized the truth; he needed to speak to Emma.

A group of men had gathered behind him, and he pushed his way through them to where he had last seen Emma, but the chair now sat empty. His heart sank as he glanced around the ballroom in search of her in the sea of people.

"You, there," Lucas called out to an older man with more hair in his mustaches than on the top of his head.

"Yes, Your Grace?" the man asked. "It is an honor to be in your presence this fine evening—"

Lucas had no time, or patience, to deal with this man, who was well-known to seek the good graces of those with wealth in order to grow his own. "Have you seen Lord Miggs?"

He shook his head, but the man beside him, a Lord Matthew Campbell if he remembered correctly, said, "He left not five minutes ago."

"Was he alone?" Lucas asked, attempting to hide his disappointment.

"No. I believe a woman was in his company."

"Thank you," Lucas said. He moved over to the refreshment table and picked up a new glass of wine. Perhaps this was a sign that he was to give up, that she did not need him after all.

"Lucas!" Ingrid said as she hurried up to him. She wore a worried expression that made his heart pound.

"What is it?"

"Oh, Lucas, I was wrong," she said as tears filled her eyes. "I was so wrong."

"What?" Lucas demanded. "Of what do you speak?"

"The baron. He was bragging to Lord Tritant about blackmailing Miss Barrington!"

"Blackmail?" Lucas asked. She was not of the *ton*; how could he blackmail her?

Ingrid swallowed hard, clearly finding the telling distasteful. "There was talk of her father being dead. He threatened to expose her unless she agreed to allow him to court her as well as give him half her father's business."

Bright light filled the room as lightning struck just outside the door to the garden, and a collective gasp resounded in the room. As if a reflection of the brewing storm, Lucas felt an anger that went well beyond anything he had ever felt. His temper had destroyed many things in his life, including giving Emma the opportunity to reach out to him.

What a fool he had been thinking only of himself and not of the woman for whom he cared. His father had been wrong, there was no longer any doubt. Those who cared only for themselves were meant to end up like his father: bitter and alone.

"Lucas?" Ingrid called out as he hurried away. "Where are you going?"

"To get the woman I love!" he called back over his shoulder.

Chapter Twenty-Three

The carriage jostled by the wind scared Emma almost as much as the drunken baron who sat beside her on the cushioned seat. After sitting alone for nearly three hours while Lord Miggs drank and made merry, she was relieved when he said they would be leaving.

Few came near her the entire night, besides the short encounter with Lucas, of course. How fortunate that she had not been expected to make small talk with people who looked at her like she was some sort of paltry insect they had found in the bedroom corner.

Now, Lord Miggs rambled on beside her as the storm continued to rage outside. "Four new accounts agreed out of the six," he slurred with a laugh. "Did I not tell you I would secure them?" He stared at her with reddened eyes, and his breath reeked of liquor.

"Yes, my lord," Emma murmured, ignoring the man's leers. "Although, I wish that perhaps next time I might be able to discuss the matters with you beforehand?"

The baron gave a hearty laugh as the carriage hit a hole in the road, causing him to fall against her. Or rather he used it as an excuse to move in closer to her. He pulled his arm onto the bench behind her and pressed his leg against hers.

"You are to work in the office, since you are the one who has the experience with the bookkeeping," he said. "Leave the business to me. After all, I must do my part to earn my half of what the business acquires."

Emma stifled a sigh. It was not only the deal he had forced upon her that frustrated her at the moment. He had also ruined the opportunity to speak to Lucas at the party. The chances of seeing him again were low, and that hurt worse than all the rest that had gone wrong in her life combined.

As Lord Miggs continued to speak, Emma inched toward the door, but he simply followed her. Then he reached out and took her hand in his.

"My lord," she said, surprised her voice was not shaking, "we must discuss our business arrangement." They had little more to discuss, but it gave her an opportunity to move his mind from whatever roguish plans he might have had. "May we meet sometime next week?"

The carriage came to a stop in front of the office, but the baron did not seem to notice. "We can discuss your concerns now if you would like." He leaned over her and opened the door. "Let us go into your…nay, *our* office."

Emma sighed. "Very well." She stepped out and shivered, although it was not the cool air that brought on such a response. Having this man at her side made panic well up inside her. As she fumbled with the keys, he reached past her with his own.

"Did you forget that, as your landlord, I had a key, as well?"

The fact this man could have entered her home at any time had never occurred to her, and now she was appalled as she wondered how many times he had done so without her knowledge. She did not put it past him to do such a thing now that she had gotten to know him better.

Once inside, she lit several candles as the rain intensified, the pounding against the window echoing in the room. Behind her, she heard the lock slide into place.

"Now, what is it you wish to discuss," he asked, removing his coat and hanging it on one of the pegs beside the door.

Emma lit two more candles and turned toward the baron. Something inside told her to wait, to delay their conversation. These games, this blackmail, had gone on long enough, and she was the only one who could put a stop to it all.

She reached out and touched her father's desk, and for a moment she saw the smile her father always wore. It was as if he spoke to her, and for a moment, she closed her eyes, remembering one of the last conversations they had shared.

"No matter what happens with the business," he had said, his voice weak, "you must be happy. Never sacrifice happiness for me, for the business, or for anyone. Do you understand?"

"I will not," she had promised, and now she understood that something far more valuable than the business existed: her happiness.

She opened her eyes, the old strength she had known before returning. It had not been her father's mission in life for Emma to run this business. No, he only wished for her to be happy. If she were destined to live the life of a beggar, then so be it, but she would put a stop to the arrangement she had made with Lord Miggs despite where it landed her.

Emma turned to find the baron staggering toward her, and she took a step back only to press against the desk. If she had thought his grin disconcerting before, it now chilled her to the bone. "My lord?" she whispered.

"Yes?" he asked as he came to a stop before her.

"Our arrangement," she stammered as she grasped at the courage that tried to fail her, "I no longer want it."

The smile the baron wore fell, and he narrowed his eyes at her. "What is this you say?"

"I am sorry, but it is not fair to me."

"How so?" he demanded.

"It was never my intention to join you in business," she explained, although speaking every word was like forcing a horse through the smallest of holes. "Yet you threatened me, and I felt obliged."

The rain continued to pound the window, but Emma's heart seemed to drown the sound as the baron began to undo the buttons on his waistcoat, his eyes burning with lust.

Looking around, Emma wished Stephen was there, or anyone else for that matter.

"So, you wish the *ton* to learn about your father, do you?" he whispered as he undid another button. "Is that what you want, you ungrateful trollop?"

"No," she managed to gasp. "I do not want that." As he threw aside the waistcoat and tugged open his shirt, anger replaced her fear. How dare he treat her in this manner! "I wish only to be treated with respect!" she shouted. "If you choose to tell anyone about my father, I cannot stop you. Regardless, our agreement is over!"

Her breathing was heavy as Lord Miggs reached out and grabbed hold of her shoulders. He looked angrier than she had ever seen him before. "You will continue to do business with me," he said, a sneer on his lips. "Not only that, but you will marry me."

"Marry you?" Emma asked in shock. "I most certainly will not..." Her words were cut off when he kissed her, his cold lips sending repulsion through her body. She pummeled at his chest with her fists, but she might have been a fly landing on a cow for all he took notice.

When he pulled away, his gaze met hers. "You will learn to love me," he whispered, and when she went to scream, his lips covered hers once again, and terror like none she had ever felt in her life raged in her as she realized what he intended for her at that moment.

***

Lucas ran to the stables, his head bent to the strong wind and steady rain. The stable boy rose from his place just inside the door, but Lucas gave him no time to speak a greeting.

"Ready the fastest horse," he shouted. When he saw the confusion on the boy's face, he added, "Now!"

The boy's eyes grew wide. "Yes, Yer Grace," he said before turning and running into the stables.

"Will your carriage not be needed, Your Grace?" Walburg asked as he rushed to Lucas's side. His driver knew his job well.

"Yes, I will need it," Lucas said. "Meet me at the office of Miss Barrington. You remember where it is?" It was a silly question, for the man had been there numerous times to collect Emma, but Lucas asked despite this fact.

"Yes, Your Grace. I do."

"Good. Leave now and wait for me there."

The man bowed and hurried away just as the stable boy walked out with a large chestnut thoroughbred with large flank muscles.

"This one belongs to Lord Chambers," the boy said. "It'd be the fastest steed here. But Lord Chambers is gonna be awful mad!"

Lucas took the reins from the boy, placed a foot in the stirrup, and mounted the horse with ease. "Tell him the Duke of Storms has need of it," Lucas said as he flicked the reins and pressed his heels into the animal's side.

The horse reared as a bolt of lightning struck a nearby tree, the booming thunder deafening, and Lucas ducked forward to keep himself from being flung from the back of the animal. As an expert horseman, he took little time to get the horse back under control before urging it forward. With each hoof-beat, the rain increased and the wind grew stronger. Lucas clung to the animal with all he had, his head bent over the horse's neck as he dug his heels into its flanks.

Although the words Ingrid had shared had been few, he had already pieced together what must have happened with Emma and Lord Miggs. The baron was not one known for his integrity, and if Lucas had kept his mind clear, he would have seen what the man had planned. The baron had clearly seen the predicament Emma was in and became greedy.

When he learned that Emma had been lying to her clients, or rather the clients of her father, about where Mr. Barrington had gone, he used that as a means to blackmail Emma. This allowed Lord Miggs the opportunity to take over the business. The situation also explained why Emma had chosen to go to dinner with the baron rather than appearing at Bonehedge Estate. It was why she wore a dress that could have only been purchased with money given to her by Lord Miggs.

Why had she not told Lucas what was happening?

The answer to that question was a simple one; Lucas had lost his temper with the woman, something he had sworn never to do again. Yet, in that broken promise, he had sent Emma down a path of suffering, and therefore, he was partly to blame for the decisions she had made.

Lucas urged the horse to move faster despite the danger of riding in the near darkness that surrounded him. If it had been even an hour later, it would have been too dark to travel, let alone to travel at the speed at which he rode now.

Water streamed into his boots, and his clothes clung to his body, for he had not taken time to throw a cloak over his shoulders or place a hat on his head. His coat was not much protection against the deluge that fell upon him, and he had to wipe water from his eyes time and again in order to clear his vision. In his heart, he cared nothing for his own comfort, for no man or beast — or weather for that matter — would prevent him from telling Emma what was on his heart.

Fields rushed by, and soon he entered the village of Rumsbury. There, he yelled to urge the horse to move even faster. Soon, the office came into sight, the carriage in front of it sending a jolt of worry into his mind. A soft glow of candlelight wafted from the window, but he could see nothing inside as he brought the horse to a halt beside the carriage he recognized as one belonging to Lord Miggs.

So, he is here with her? Lucas thought. *Well, he will get a taste of the ire of the Duke of Storms!*

Throwing the reins over a nearby post, Lucas jumped from the horse and peered through the window. If he had been angry before, he was now furious, for what he saw made his blood boil. Emma stood, her eyes wide with terror. Then she screamed as the baron pressed against her, forcing her against the desk as her scream was cut off by his mouth covering hers.

In that moment, the wind surged and lightning illuminated everything around Lucas. The words Emma spoke to him weeks before entered his mind, and they could not have been truer than they were at this very moment.

"The anger that resides inside you?" she asked. "Do you know its cause?"

He sighed. "I do. Yet, whenever it comes to mind, it makes my anger increase tenfold. I would say it is a curse. Would you agree?"

"If you allow it to control you, then yes, I could name it as such. Yet it can also be a blessing."

"A blessing?" he asked, chuckling. "How could what makes me angry be a blessing?"

"It is a spark," Emma explained, "that could be used for good."

That spark ignited something deep inside him, and finding the door locked, he raised his foot and thrust it forward.

***

Emma could not stop the deluge of tears that ran down her cheeks as she stared at the man leering down at her. She wanted to spit out the taste of his mouth upon hers, but the thought of angering him further terrified her. With his body pressed against her, she could not have moved let alone gotten away to safety. Furthermore, he was a baron; how far would she be forced to go to be safe from this man?

"Now, let us go to your room," he said in a husky voice. "I am sure your bed is as good as any for what I would like to do with you."

The roar of what sounded much like a crazed animal made the baron pause, but the crash of splintering wood made them both jump, and Emma looked toward the door just as a flash of lightning highlighted the silhouette of a man where the door had once been.

"What the...?" Lord Miggs pulled away from Emma and spun toward the door. "Your Grace?"

The baron had just enough time to address Lucas before Lucas grabbed him by the coat and slammed his fist into the man's stomach. The baron had no time to react to that strike when his jaw cracked from a second.

Lucas pulled the baron until his face was inches from that of Lucas. "How dare you!" he said through clenched teeth. "You mean to hurt her?"

"Never!" the baron managed to gasp. "I-I am sorry."

Lucas pulled his arm back, ready to strike the man again, but Emma rushed over. "No, Lucas," she begged. "No more. I am safe now."

The duke seemed to hesitate, but then Lord Miggs began to weep.

Emma had no pity for the man who had attacked her, but she also did not wish to see Lucas lose all he had accomplished over the past few weeks. In her estimation, he had worked too hard to return to the man he had been because of her. "Calm the storm," she whispered.

Lucas blinked and then lowered his fist to his side, although he continued to hold the baron by his coat. "What you have done to this woman is abhorrent," Lucas seethed. "How dare you blackmail her and attempt to take over her business? But to assault her? That goes beyond reprehensible. You are lower than the vermin that dine on scraps in the road."

"I am sorry!" the baron cried. "I beg your forgiveness. I will make this right. What price must I pay? Name it! Anything, and I will pay!"

Lucas turned toward Emma. "What do you think?"

"I do not know," she said, her heart still beating so strongly against her chest she worried it would burst from her breast at any moment. She was not thinking clearly enough to make any decisions at the moment. "You decide."

Lucas pushed the baron away as he released his grip. "You will return home this evening and gather a week's worth of clothing and nothing more. I will come to your estate tomorrow morning. If you are still there, or if I hear a rumor of you being near Rumsbury, you will find your debt to be more than your home."

Lord Miggs' eyes grew wide with surprise, and Lucas leaned forward, his nose within inches of the baron's.

"Do not doubt my ability to call down lightning upon you," he whispered just as a flash lit up the street.

"It is true!" the baron screeched as he ran from the office. "He does control the weather! May God save us all!" Then he jumped into the waiting carriage and was soon gone.

Chapter Twenty-Four

E mma stared in silence as the carriage carrying the baron moved down the street. When she returned her gaze to Lucas, she was shocked to see water dripping from his clothing. He had no hat or overcoat, and by the flickering light of the candle, if she did not know him, she would not have recognized him as a member of the *ton*.

"Are you all right?" he asked, his face filled with concern.

"Yes," she replied. Then the reality of what had happened came crashing down around her, and she shook her head at the recent memory. "He tried...he is a disgusting man!" Lord Miggs might as well have struck her in the stomach with the amount of pain Emma felt. Soon, she was trembling in the arms of Lucas as she sobbed into his chest. What would have happened if Lucas had not arrived when he did? Just the thought of what might have been made her weep all the harder.

"Shh," he whispered as he kissed the top of her head. "It is over now. No one will ever hurt you again."

When the tears receded, she pulled away from his embrace and looked up at him. "How...how did you know to come here?" she asked. "And why are you here?"

"I wanted to speak to you again. When I learned you had left the party, I..." His words trailed off, and he looked at the ground, the shame on his face clear. "I regretted how I spoke to you. I knew something was not right, but I ignored my instincts. If it had not been for Ingrid coming to me because of what Lord Tritant had heard..."

"What did he hear?"

"That the baron has been blackmailing you," Lucas replied. "He admitted it outright. Then Lord Tritant told Ingrid, who came to me right away." He looked down at her. "That plus the concerns I already had solidified my suspicions that things were not as they seemed."

Emma sighed. "It is true. I should have told you, but I feared you would think I was taking advantage of you. When it came to the point I knew I had to tell you, I was unable to."

"You could never take advantage of me," he whispered as he moved a lock of hair that had fallen loose from her coiffure. "The fault lies with me. A man does not lose his temper and shout at someone for whom he cares." He took her hands in his and shook his head in wonder. "You have taught me so much in such a short time. The truth is, I need you in my life. I am sorry for everything."

She brushed away a stray tear. "I need you, as well," she said with a small smile. "I found myself not only caring for you very deeply, but I also realize it is something stronger and even more special."

He raised a single eyebrow. "Oh? And what is that?"

"I learned that I love you."

Then Lucas leaned down and pressed his lips to hers. Unlike the harshness of Lord Miggs, this kiss was as soft and beautiful as she had imagined it to be.

When the kiss ended, Lucas smiled. "I love you as well," he said. Did he sound as breathless as Emma felt? "Never again will I lash out at you in anger. I will listen and learn."

Emma heaved a sigh of relief. "I am glad, for your anger is much like the whip of a flogger," she teased.

He gave her a mock gasp of shock. Then he softened his features. "Then I promise I will speak openly to you rather than waiting to build any anger I might have."

"That is a good start," she replied with a smile. Then she looked at his dripping clothes. "I have some of Father's clothes upstairs. If you do not mind wearing clothing that was not made by your tailor, that is."

"I would not mind if it means I will be dry," he said with a light shiver. "I will build a fire."

She went upstairs and found several articles of clothing for him. In the office, she could hear him placing logs in the fireplace and the flick of the flint and steel. Soon, the slight smell of smoke wafted in the air.

Once Lucas had changed — she giggled when he went upstairs to do so — she poured them each a cup of tea. When he returned, they each placed a chair in front of the now roaring fire.

They sat in silence for some time, each in his or her own thoughts as they stared into the dancing flames. Lucas's hair still shone with dampness, but he had removed the wet ribbon and now his locks lay on his shoulders. Emma thought she had never seen such a handsome man in her life and doubted she ever would again.

"So, tell me about your father," Emma said in an attempt to break the silence.

Lucas snorted. "My father," he repeated. "Well, he was a man who taught me all I know, including my propensity for anger…"

As Emma listened, she filed away each piece of information, for she knew that the more information she had, the more she could help him ease the anger that still simmered inside. A simple promise would not keep him from erupting, but over time, he would learn to put that energy to better use. Anger had its place — she had learned as much in the past week. Misplaced anger only caused hurt rather than helped. And she would do what she could to help him reach that potential.

As the hour passed and they each shared more about their lives, Emma had to force her eyes to remain open. Lucas must have noticed, for he placed his cup on a nearby table and stood. "You should go to bed," he said. Emma went to protest, but he forestalled her with a raise of his hand. "No, I see how weary you are. Walburg and I will remain here to keep guard, just in case Miggs decides to return. He was never very intelligent."

Emma sighed. "I will sleep well knowing you will comfort me," she said as he placed his hands on her waist. "Thank you. For everything."

"It is I who must thank you," Lucas whispered. "Tomorrow, the storm outside will subside, as will the one I carry within me."

Smiling, Emma lifted herself onto her toes and their lips met once more, bringing her a sense of safety and the assurance she needed to know all would be well. Not only did his eyes say as much, but the love in her heart said so, as well.

The night had begun with her filled with fear, but now it ended in love. And for the first time in over a year, she fell asleep with a smile on her lips and her heart at ease.

***

The following morning, Emma woke to bright sunlight peeking through the tiny cracks between the stones in the walls. She poured water from the pitcher and washed her face and teeth and then donned one of her old dresses. The gown she wore the night before lay in a heap in the corner, and later she would see it burned. For now, she had other issues she had to manage.

When she got to the bottom of the stairs, the duke stood beside what was left of the broken door. When he turned toward her, she giggled.

"And what makes you laugh this early in the morning?" he asked with clear amusement.

She could not help but stare at how her father's shirt clung to his muscular torso, and her stomach tightened in a strange way. Her laughter was gone, now replaced with some other new sensation, one she had never experienced before. Yet it was not unpleasant in any way.

"Nothing," she said in a hoarse whisper. When he approached, her throat seemed to tighten further.

"Nothing, you say?" he said, his voice husky. Then he leaned down and kissed her. This time, there was an urgency behind it, and she trembled in his embrace.

When the kiss ended, she was left breathless, and as her head rested against his chest, she listened to the quick pounding of his heart that matched her own. "I often wondered what it would be like to be in your arms."

He raised an eyebrow. "Do you enjoy it?"

"I do." She looked up at him and laughed. "You are smiling again."

"I suppose a man does that when he is happily in love. Did you not say my name shall be the Duke of Smiles?"

She laughed again. "I said no such thing! I believe that was you who made such a statement." She traced the angle of his jaw. "I believe it is a wonderful name. Although, I must admit that the Duke of Storms has his place in this world."

"Oh?" Lucas asked in a shocked tone. "I thought he was to be put to rest."

"If he had not arrived last night, I am unsure what would have happened. There are extreme circumstances when he is appropriate."

"As long as I control it, correct?"

She nodded. "Indeed."

"Well, I look forward to working on that control," he said. "With your help, of course."

Emma smiled. "It would be my honor."

"What is this?"

They both turned to see Stephen in the doorway, his hands on his hips and a frown on his face. "I should've known! Duke or no, I'll not let you hurt Miss Emma anymore!" He raised his fist, but Emma stepped between him and Lucas.

"It is all right," she said as she placed a hand on his arm. "I am safe, I promise."

He glanced at the broken door and then glared at Lucas. "Are you sure? He hasn't hurt you or something, has he? Look at the door!" He frowned again. "I'm not scared of him, you know!"

"I realize you are not," Emma replied, stifling a giggle. "This was all because of the baron." She indicated the door with her hand. "If it was not for Lucas...I mean His Grace, then I am unsure what would have happened."

"The baron? You mean Lord Miggs?" His frown deepened. "Just you wait 'til I see him!" He pushed a fist into his opposite palm and then shook his head as if to clear it. "I'm glad you're safe, Miss Emma."

"As am I," Emma replied and then raised her eyebrows at him with expectation.

He gave a heavy sigh and bowed. "I'm sorry for threatening you, Your Grace. Please forgive me."

Lucas smiled. "There is no need to apologize. In fact, I am the one who owes you an apology."

"Beg your pardon?" Stephen asked in shock.

Lucas nodded. "When you came to my home, you spoke of treasuring the friendship I had with Emma. I was a fool to not understand the wisdom of your words."

"Wisdom?" Stephen echoed with a scratch to his head. "That's kind of you to say, Your Grace, but I can't read nor write a lick. I think that makes me the fool."

"No, you are not a fool. You are a gentleman of the highest order, one who, just as a moment ago, is willing to take a stand for what is right. Thank you for sharing such knowledge. You are an example to many."

Stephen's cheeks reddened, and he stuttered his thanks as a man peeked into the doorway.

"We've the door you called for, Your Grace," he said.

"Wonderful," Lucas replied. "Go on then; we will stay out of your way."

It did not take him long to install the new door and remove the old, and while he worked, Lucas pulled Stephen aside to chat some more.

Emma walked over to the desk where her father once sat and ran her fingers over the rough old wood. "I did it, Father," she whispered. "I found my happiness by securing the greatest account of all times. My heart."

Epilogue

Time passed as quickly as the clouds that raced across the sky, and Emma smiled as she thought about all that had transpired over the past year. Her business was growing, and Stephen took pride in each account he secured.

The previous week, she had hired a man from London to keep the books, a man by the name of Mr. Sykes, who came highly recommended and deemed trustworthy. Stephen had taken the old room upstairs and continued to do odd jobs for the office. Emma was pleased that Mr. Sykes and Stephen got on well, for that had been one requirement she refused to ignore. As she had promised, Stephen had a place in the office for as long as he liked, and Lucas had agreed wholeheartedly.

Now, she stood in the grand ballroom of Bonehedge Estate. She looked at the small contingency of wedding guests and was pleased to see they each wore a broad smile. Their laughter filled the room, but that of Lucas outshone them all. He stood with a group of friends, including Ingrid.

The viscountess had apologized to Emma after learning what Lord Miggs had done. They had become close after that, and Emma now understood why Lucas kept the woman as such a dear friend. She had a kind heart beneath that haughty shell, and Emma believed herself lucky to have earned the woman's friendship. Although, it was Ingrid who said the same about Emma.

Lucas looked over at Emma and smiled. He said a few words to those with him and then walked over to stand beside her.

"Do you realize that you are the most beautiful bride in all of England?" he asked as he kissed her cheek.

"And you are by far the most handsome of grooms," she replied. He offered his arm, which she took without hesitation. When he walked down the path away from the party, she gave him a questioning look. "The guests?"

"They have plenty to keep them occupied," he said with a secretive smile. "We are allowed a few moments of privacy, do you not agree?"

"Oh, very much so," she answered with a giggle.

They continued down the path until they came to a stop at the fence that looked over the rolling hills beyond the garden, green with the summer weather.

"I never knew such happiness could exist until I met you," he said before turning his gaze to her. "I look forward to our many years ahead."

"As do I," Emma said.

His arms wrapped around her and drew her in, and they kissed with a passion that Emma thought would never be quenched. When the kiss ended, they turned and looked out across the hills once more, Emma glad for the moment to catch her breath.

And there they stood, together, arm in arm, their silence speaking louder than their voices. For that was the beauty of love. Love was in a whispered word or a willing ear to listen, that was true. It was also in the smile shared between two people, for her husband was now a man of smiles and patience, and the storm that once clouded their lives was gone, replaced by the sun that now shone above them.

And Emma knew it would always be so. Forever.

Author's Note

Jennifer Monroe lives part time in the state of New York and part time in Colorado and dedicates her time to her writing and her husband and two daughters.

She writes Regency romances with heart! With stories of first loves, second chances, dashing dukes, and ladies in distress, each turn of the page promises an adventure in love.

Not sure where to begin? Download her free ebook, *A Lady's Promise*, from her website – www.jennifermonroeromance.com – and have it delivered to your inbox today!

If you enjoy Regency Romances that center around siblings, you will love my nine-part series that begins with a marriage of convenience in *Whispers of Light*.

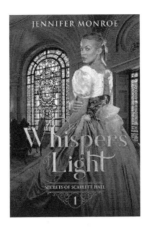

A Lady's Promise, the prequel to the Scarlett Hall series, tells of Miss Eleanor Parker's desire to wed the man she loves despite the wishes of an overbearing mother. Available for free from my website: www.jennifermonroeromance.com.

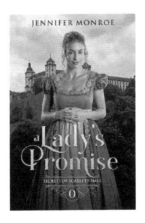

Do you enjoy a bit of 'whodunit'? Check out my Victoria Parker Regency Mysteries series. Victoria is on the hunt for a murderer when she is invited to the home of the Duke of Everton. Check out Dukes, Drinks, and Murder.

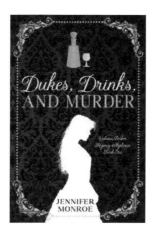

Made in the USA
Middletown, DE
20 June 2023

32881260R00104